Praise for *Caesaria*

T0278836

"A glimpse into the life of a woman
curiosity. A quietly raw, poetic study of imprisonment, both
imposed and internalized, and the shifting boundaries between
care and neglect, human kindness and human cruelty."
—Marta Balcewicz, author of *Big Shadow*

"Nordenhök's locked-up mansion is a disciplinary system of
supervision and punishment, a claustrophobic spectacle where
death and disaster are indisputable components in the condition
of being a girl. *Caesaria* is simply wonderful!"
—Johanne Lykke Holm, author of *Strega*

"A novel as beautiful as it is unsettling. Hanna Nordenhök's prose
combines with singular mastery the density of poetry with the
feverish atmosphere of a gothic tale."
—Fernanda Melchor, author of *Paradais* and *Hurricane Season*

"Frightening, alluring, full of beauty, pain, and grief."
—*Dagens Nyheter*

"A breathlessly creepy and deeply affecting portrait of a girl's
life so confined and so deprived of impressions that it's verging
on madness."
—*Göteborgs-Posten*

"A dark, violent, and at times breathtakingly beautiful tale, at the
same time as it works as a brutal account on gender and power."
—*Opulens*

"Nordenhök's prose is clean yet rhythmic, and words are used
with a precision and sensibility for their nuances that simply is
remarkable... *Caesaria* is a novel of the highest quality."
—*Svenska Dagbladet*

"Nordenhök writes sentences that are intense and ambiguous,
like sinister omens of what is to come... The furiously beautiful
sentences and the horror that lurks underneath them create an
atmosphere that recalls Marguerite Duras's portrayals of the
intimate relationship between lust and pain."
—*Sydsvenskan*

Caesaria

Hanna Nordenhök

Translated from the Swedish by Saskia Vogel

LITERATURE IN TRANSLATION SERIES
BOOK*HUG PRESS
TORONTO 2024

First North American English Edition
Original text © 2020 by Hanna Nordenhök; first published by
Norstedts, Sweden
Translation © 2024 by Saskia Vogel

This edition published by arrangement with Norstedts Agency and
Héloïse Press

Library and Archives Canada Cataloguing in Publication

Title: Caesaria / Hanna Nordenhök ; translated by Saskia Vogel.
Other titles: Caesaria. English
Names: Nordenhök, Hanna, 1977- author. | Vogel, Saskia, translator.
Series: Literature in translation series.
Description: First Canadian edition. | Series statement: Literature in
translation series |
    Translation of Caesaria. | In English, translated from the Swedish.
Identifiers: Canadiana (print) 20240345606 | Canadiana (ebook)
20240345622
    ISBN 9781771669122 (softcover)
    ISBN 9781771669153 (EPUB)
Subjects: LCGFT: Gothic fiction. | LCGFT: Novels.
Classification: LCC PT9877.24.O728 C3413 2024 | DDC 839.73/8—dc23

Book*hug Press acknowledges that the land on which we operate is
the traditional territory of many nations, including the Mississaugas
of the Credit, the Anishnabeg, the Chippewa, the Haudenosaunee,
and the Wendat peoples. We recognize the enduring presence of many
diverse First Nations, Inuit, and Métis peoples, and are grateful for the
opportunity to meet, work, and learn on this territory.

To AP, with love

Everything in woman is a riddle
—FRIEDRICH NIETZSCHE

IT WAS THE NIGHT little Beda and I took to the forest that I realized I'd never be able to leave Lilltuna and the room with the East Indian wall clock. Its steely eye would stare back at me forever. And I'd never learn anything other than what I had learned there.

Snow now.

I sleep with my body pressed to the stove; I've laid out all the objects so I can see them. The cold crackles in the tiles. At dusk the animals draw nearer to the house; they're seeking heat and food. At first they stand at the edge of the forest, trampling, then they grow bolder. Come daybreak, a hazy sun.

Snow.

The pond in the forest was also like an eye when Beda and I drew near it at dawn, the morning after we'd taken to the woods. It was like in my dream, but without the flames. Late summer. The eye was grey and still, framed by cattails and reeds, a liquid pupil: perhaps it had always been watching us. The edge of trees on the far bank steamed in the gritty light. A distant fox. I was wearing my wadmal trousers, I was wielding the Sceptre, my body was Bandaged and Bound. A streak of autumn through the August air. Beda complained. *We're almost there,* I said, coaxing her now. I offered her my hand. A bird screeched. Then the sky broke open and the sun's flaming orb lit up the pines, its light corroding the tangle of branches. We had arrived. And yet we'd got nowhere. And it was clear to me: we had got nowhere.

Then morning arrived, and we were retrieved.

It was my twelfth birthday.

The first thing I learned was Lilltuna, and Lilltuna belonged to Doctor Eldh.

Wattle fences criss-crossing the wetlands. Magpies above the trees. The smell of young turnips and the cat shit in the cellar.

I learned the nails in the barn walls, I learned my knuckles, I learned the moonlight pooling on the floor tiles in my nursery on clear wintry nights. I learned every inch of the square piano, too: I sat on the screw stool with its embroidered carnations, I wore the yellow dress with the puffed sleeves, I played the polka and "Für Elise." The keys were already cracked and veined like an old person's fingers.

I learned the keys, I learned the screw stool.

During my Saturday baths, down in the kitchen, after my body had been lowered into the steaming tub, I always sat stiff and upright while my still-damp hair was set in tight braids: outside, the infinite evenings. Night birds volleyed messages until I drifted off.

The first and last thing I learned was Lilltuna. I slept, I woke, I played with my dolls: outside was the forest. Now and then that particular light fell across the barn and the pasture, a yellow-streaked, savage blush, as if to remind me that Lilltuna was chosen and blessed. When the toys in my nursery broke, I simply added them to the wish list I kept in the lockable drawer in the little nightstand, making sure to cross out the old entries each time before handing it to Doctor Eldh. New toys would always arrive to replace the discarded ones.

After Beda and I were retrieved from the pond in the forest that morning, I was tucked back in with the old horse blanket in the nursery. My knees chafed against the wool through the linen. I smelled of forest and rotten apples; I watched the late-summer flies slowly die between the double set of windows. On my sixteenth day of bedrest, Doctor Eldh arrived.

He came from the city in a hired cabriolet; he sat in the rattan armchair at the foot of the bed; he steepled his fingers. The armrests groaned under his great elbows. Slender pulsing veins at his temples, his jaw tense beneath those billowing whisker-clouds. I leaned on him, half-squinting, my eyelids reluctant and heavy, as if the forest's enchanting air was still trembling against my face, just as it had against Beda's and mine that morning in the glowing light, at the edge of the universe. He was disappointed, that much was clear. His feet were restless. A red-tinged evening light lay upon his high, untroubled brow. I listened to the silences before his words, to the rowan's windblown branches whipping the nursery window. The smell of old Mam'selle Fanny's coffee rose from the ground floor. I turned to face the wall, I let him begin. He spoke the same words he always had, tasting them, enticing himself with them so they sounded unexpected and new, though the story he told was the same: the story of my Creation. His forehead in the light, the armchair's gentle groan. The words like a crystal of rock sugar about to burst on his tongue. Then: How the woman who would soon become my mother had come to him in distress. How the cabriolets had skidded across the cobblestones in the golden summer rain, outside the city's lying-in hospital. How in the light of the oil lamp, that scrawny, shabbily dressed woman's swollen abdomen, its web of veins close to the surface of her stretched skin, had taken on a deep blue sheen: later, too, when she was already dead, how her belly had appeared to ferment and turn blue, how her body had lain there on the bed in a stream of daylight, by then opened and emptied and sewn back up with sturdy catgut sutures.

The rainlight, the clang of instruments in the enamel bowls. Later: how he cut me out and into life, as one lifts a shimmering pearl from an oyster.

Sometime after that, he took me to Lilltuna.

My nursery at Lilltuna as a child: the closed dollhouse made of blue-stained pine, the ruby-rose box full of pine cones and rocks—all that was allowed to remain long after I'd stopped playing with them. Moths swarming around the sooty glass of the bedside lamp. Krantz out in the pasture, weaving between the bony backs of the dairy cows, which gleamed in Lilltuna's pink dusk as it slowly reeled back into the pitch-black night.

I played hopscotch on the pavement under the linden trees, behind the main house; I walked on stilts between the cow pats in the pasture: I was three years old, I was six, then eight. I skated on the little ice rinks Krantz would make for me by tipping out several barrels of meltwater onto the gravel next to the barn, ahead of the next deep freeze: I waited for Doctor Eldh, for him to return from the city and give me my lessons at the walnut writing desk, under the East Indian wall clock in the library. I slept, I played, I memorized the alphabet, etiquette, the names of countries. Through the walls I heard Mam'selle Fanny and the maids, their voices as light and sharp as a magpie's wing, Krantz's steps down on the gravel, the animals bleating and bellowing. Fanny's smell in my nostrils, though ever more distant now. The sudden silences of the birds in the trees outside, as if the landscape were inexplicably holding its breath.

I added to my wish list, I got everything I asked for.

The rowan branches thick with snow outside my window. The rowan in bloom, the rowan bent with the weight of berries, the rowan dressed in autumn's every hue. I practised arithmetic in my little book and spelling at the school desk in the nursery; I was given straight or looped braids; I was dressed in pinafores. I was already an Incurable One, but I didn't know that yet. Later, when I understood, I became the Bandaged One.

Dusks gave way to dawns.

Glimmers of light came and vanished.

Beda and I could easily have continued into the pond early that morning, out into the grey eye that opened there between the trees and seemed to have us in its sight. We could have crossed to the other side. To whatever was out there, beyond Lilltuna's end. We could have walked on, into the forest, lived there, eating sorrel and drinking spring water.

But we didn't; we stayed where we were at the water's edge. Until the prickle of daylight came, and Krantz suddenly appeared, there between the spruce trees, and I released my grip on Beda, and we allowed ourselves to be retrieved.

Maybe it really had been the badger that screamed on those summer nights, maybe the screams had not been Beda's but the badger's, but for some reason the animal had stayed silent on the night we took to the woods. And I wonder if any of what followed that winter, the winter during which the one who called himself Master Valdemar arrived at Lilltuna, would have happened had I not discovered my morbid disposition. The disease that had begun in one location, only to spread, which is when I'd started beating it into submission with tightly wound bandages.

After he arrived, the one who called himself Master Valdemar slept; he slept, his smooth face framed by his fair curls; he slept through February. He lay behind the closed library doors, his weakened body warming up between the furs and bolsters of the guest bed that had been placed under the East Indian wall clock. His green eyes were concealed by those finely wrought eyelids. He had been brought here by Doctor Eldh. The fields and the pasture under a blanket of snow. The spruce tops sharp against a leaden sky.

But at long last spring did come, and the master was roused from his deep slumber. And he rose from the bed that Mam'selle Fanny had made for him at Doctor Eldh's behest.

Summer came, summer went.

And the lingonberries gleamed in the sunshine, and Master Valdemar slept no more.

DOCTOR HENRY ALEXIUS ELDH cut me from his scrawny one's belly. Then he took me to Lilltuna. Perhaps he had simply dreamed of going about his work undisturbed, of a far-flung outpost where he could enjoy a spell of solitude or just somehow be forgiven: for, after all, he was a man who fished for pearls.

He would come to tell me so much. As far back as I can remember, I would sit at the desk in Doctor Eldh's library, listening to his stories. I received them like a well receives the few shiny coins tossed into it, as if I were an opening that the words could slowly sail through, down to its murky bottom.

The library was sparsely furnished, with shelves along the walls that the doctor never filled. Sporadically, he'd lose his train of thought mid-sentence, which made me wonder if he remembered I was there. But then he'd look at me, dazed and thankful, as the evening light came through the tall windows, streaking the room and his large face red.

He would come to tell me so much.

Such as how, over in the city, he'd stood in the operating theatre's glaring light, by his scrawny one's bed, and observed that rigid body. How he'd seen to it that she was administered chamomile tea enemas, then chloroform, and powder to calm her on waking. Nonetheless she'd lain, stiff and dead, turning blue before him in the next day's sun, and the rain had stopped.

Doctor Eldh told and retold the story of how I came into the world. He told it on my birthday, he told it at Christmas, and I collected the words inside my head or in the small notebooks he brought me from the city. He was fond of details, such as the fact that the night before the operation his scrawny one had sat on the bed, rocking violently throughout the preliminary examination. Her eyes were pale blue, liquidy, specked yellow near her dilated pupils. She hissed or stayed silent in response to his questions, the rain continually pattering on the windows; she had screamed herself hoarse trying to give birth to me over the previous days. Not only was her body frail and scrawny, her pelvis was also malformed. Early on, the idea of drawing the child out with forceps had been rejected and a cut had seemed inevitable. The doctor had consulted the literature, not having performed the procedure himself, and seen to it that ice and freshly boiled sponges were set out: he'd had the messenger boy summon his colleagues and interested students at the medical school. He'd informed the patient of the courses of action available to her in light of the malformed pelvis: surgery, or the dismemberment of the fetus with sharp instruments. At first, the scrawny one's eyes had skidded across the walls and the growing mass of onlookers. Yellow, watery. Then she had agreed to the cut. Even as she was anaesthetized, she had tossed about, which made the opening of the abdomen more difficult, but, thanks to the determined intervention of two student assistants, the womb was fixed in place and intestinal prolapse prevented.

Doctor Eldh then made several small incisions in the exposed uterus, and jets of blood the length of quill feathers had spurted from it.

The anaesthetized woman had then suffered a severe and prolonged contraction of the uterus, and sponges were pressed against the bowels to stem the hemorrhaging: when the contractions subsided, the uterus was cut right through, and the lifeless little creature, covered in birthing custard, who was me, could be plucked out and resuscitated, by means of insufflation and cold compresses.

After, in the first hours of the day, the scrawny one had lain wide awake, her wound gaping. She was given three doses of ergot and brandy in broth, and an iron chloride solution was applied to the placenta wall, then a block of ice was placed inside her to encourage the uterus to close. Her liquid gaze had continued to skid around the room: I was presented to her but she had been distant and uncomprehending. More powders were administered. The open wound was closed with sturdy sutures. As the day proceeded, gases formed inside her—the result of chloroform or mental agitation, it was thought.

August gave way to September. For days, intervals of heavy late-summer rain had given the apricot-coloured buildings opposite the lying-in hospital a golden shimmer. Doctor Eldh's desk sat by one of the windows that faced the street, and on it stood small oval portraits of his daughters and dead wife, all three smiling with closed mouths under flat straw hats trimmed with black silk ribbons. Later, he'd transport the framed ovals to Lilltuna, along with a number of other desk items and sundries he needed close at hand: he'd place the ovals on the sideboard in the library, under the East Indian wall clock, where, during my lessons, the pictures inside them watched me from behind their domed glass fronts. But before that, the doctor had sat at his desk at the hospital and drafted his case studies and his reports for the Royal Health Collegium. He had the deceased sent for autopsy, and then the body's narrow pelvis was measured and weighed, and, once cleaned, archived in the university's collection of pathological skel- etal remains. Some time later, just as he had done with the three oval portraits, the doctor would bring its pubis to Lilltuna, plucking it from the collection so he could scruti- nize it for a paper he was working on. After that, the pubis remained there, locked in the right-hand drawer of the walnut desk, still in the university's cardboard box, labelled *No. 38*.

I used to imagine how, after my arrival in this world, the doctor might have stood in front of the small mirror in the lying-in hospital's cloakroom and considered his large face, childish somehow in its roundness. Later, he would look for evidence that my birth was among the more extraordinary of previous cuts, both the documented cases and those he'd heard tell of. Perhaps, there in the mirror, he'd have run a hand over his head, the hair already thinning, as he met his own gaze behind the glass. Perhaps on his shirt collar he had spotted a barely perceptible spatter of blood from the operation the night before but had let it be, as the shirt was otherwise ironed and clean, and had put on his top hat, left the building, and made the short walk to the Eldh residence, or the Society of Sciences, a few streets away.

I often wondered about the doctor's life over there in the city: how the colour of the sky might have shifted above the rooftops on his walks home from the hospital and Society gatherings, and how his two daughters might have moved around in their rooms, behind their windows and walls and wallpaper, and what their faces were like, and the colours of their eyes and hair. Early on, I learned which questions could and could not be asked; if I asked the right ones, the answers would be mine.

What is the purpose of the human skeleton, Doctor Eldh? I asked.

The skeleton is the hard structure that holds one erect, he answered.

How does one sleep and eat in the city, Doctor Eldh? I asked.

One eats simply and sleeps in narrow beds, in dwellings stacked on top of each other like boxes, he answered.

But how is it possible for the human body to be opened up and then closed again? I asked.

Through the manufacture of appropriate instruments in the service of scientific precision, he answered.

He came to tell me so much, and always the same stories, though with slight variations and renewed emphases: how, the day after the cut, he had chased away the poor relief when they came for the child who was me; how he had taken me under his wing and assumed responsibility for my upbringing; how he had bought a summer residence where I was to be looked after and educated, a great, white-rendered manor house shaded by giant poplars, linden trees, witch hazel, and rowan. Below it lay a field, and an English garden with an arbour and flagstone paths, and a small hexagonal copper-domed gazebo nestled between bird cherry and pear trees; further off there were barns, sheds, wells, a farmhand's cottage, and an old wooden building where a mangle was kept. And the garden quickly became overgrown, the vegetation unruly. The doctor said it was love at first sight with the rendered house, which turned fiery yellow in the evening sun; in those evenings he'd sit in the gazebo wrapped in blankets, reading while the roe deer moved in restless flocks through the garden. Up in the nursery, the child who was me would be fast asleep, her tiny eyelids twitching. The house lay secluded, behind the marshes that carved their way through the landscape and the forests beyond. A small private road briefly followed the edge of one of the fields before ending at the top of a hill, and, from the house, it wasn't possible to see the slopes beyond the crest of that hill, with their isolated homesteads, and more numerous fields, and their roads running through the landscape toward distant towns and villages. Not far into the forested land that lay inside the estate was the pond, a bathing pond, long since abandoned, with its wooden dock for washing and a sunken rowboat still tied to a post: across the pond was the property's boundary, where a new stretch of forest reached into the landscape.

The estate could be reached from the city via a comfortable two-hour carriage journey. The doctor would keep the top up on his way out, composing his case studies and drafting remarks for Society gatherings as he travelled through woods and meadows in the wan pink light. He hired a housekeeper to oversee both the estate and me, along with a farmhand and later a succession of maids, who peered at him with watery eyes from under their work caps as they sat with their porridge in the kitchen. Their searching glances, and the rumours that began to reach the doctor's ears when he was out in the city, would in time make him take greater care with his choice of maid, and there were to be as few as possible. But the farm was also to be self-sufficient, with cows, sheep, and chickens, requiring several pairs of nimble hands. And less frequent trips to the city for supplies. When the doctor alighted from his carriage at the entrance to the house, the housekeeper was to be on the front steps with the child, who would immediately come toddling toward him.

I had yellow eyes, I had hair as brown as silky clay, my palms were pink and always open. The doctor might have hoped for an outpost in which to preserve a pearl. And had he not rescued this child from the gutter? Indeed, he had. And out there the world was twisted and dark. The workhouses were crowded, and the girls in them starved, growing ugly and imprudent and hollowed-out on the road to perdition. He had wanted to protect me, he said. And so he had kept me.

I was given three names: Henrietta Alexia Caesaria. The first and second after him, and the last for the cut, through which he'd plucked me from the darkness.

And then there was the night I took to the forest, which was of course a disappointment.

WHEN I WAS A small child, I often asked myself why Doctor Eldh kept me out at Lilltuna, even though he did do his best to explain; now I no longer wonder.

During his visits, he'd sometimes take me out into the countryside surrounding the estate, in a cabriolet, so I could get some fresh air; he'd clamp his gold-framed pince-nez to the bridge of his nose and read aloud to me from the *Flora* so I would learn to identify animals and plants. The coachmen who drove us were from the city, and different every time, and they never turned their heads; I'd watch their shoulders move under their coats or shirts as they handled the reins. The blue, blush, white summer skies. The doctor would sit next to me, the book open on his lap. The sun's glare would fall upon that big face of his, his ice-grey whiskers casting talon-like shadows on his collar: I could have reached out and touched that high, untroubled forehead. I repeated the names of plant parts; I studied the book's illustrations while the doctor dozed under his top hat on the way home; I let the breeze cool my face. From the woods across a ditch rose the sickly sweet scent of withering blooms and dead deer. Sometimes we saw people in the distance, children on wattle fences, hay carts. Then, Doctor Eldh would tap the coach box with his walking stick, and we'd turn around.

I suppose the doctor thought that Lilltuna would stay as it was. The scudding clouds above the bird cherry trees. The cows in the pasture. The lambs in the pen. The child that was me, sleeping or playing in the nursery he had furnished on the top floor of the big white house.

He came and he left in a steady rhythm. He draped his frock coat over the back of the armchair and sat across from me at the walnut desk under the wall clock, his early-reader books spread out for me on the tabletop. He let me lie on the Persian rug and make charcoal drawings on the rose-scented paper he brought me from the city, while he worked by the light of his desk lamp, late into the evening, and the small flame inside the green glass cylinder began to waver and die.

I often asked him about things I'd never seen.

What are cobblestones, Doctor Eldh? I asked.

The stones are laid to support the movement of carriages, draft animals, and people travelling by foot, he replied.

What are the lanterns in the city like, Doctor Eldh? I asked.

Like fireflies in the dark, replied the doctor.

I'd write down the unfamiliar words in the notebooks he brought to Lilltuna, recording each new one, and once they'd been repeated often enough and become imprinted on my memory, I'd cross them out, one by one, so I would become one with the knowledge he imparted. I sat on the chair across the table from the doctor; I was a pearl or a well, a treasure, a precipice.

Sometimes, in the evening, when I was in bed, I heard a voice in my head, mingling with Mam'selle Fanny's as she read to me about the Lord Jesus Christ while I drifted off. The voice was bright and piercing, an otherworldly sound, it belonged to Doctor Eldh.

And the pond hadn't been all that far away, the time I took Beda with me into the summer night. And the creatures had darted around us in the dark, pine martens with acrid coats whistling past our feet in the undergrowth. I was the Bandaged One. I held the Sceptre all the way, even if I did almost drop it. It was out in the marshland at the foot of the hill where Beda fell down. She wouldn't move, refused to get up, and I had to pull at her arms and clothing to drag her along. That's when I repeated the final instruction to myself:

And there appeared a sign in the firmament: a woman, clothed with the sun, toiling in childbirth. And behold: a great red dragon came and, with its tail, swept half the stars out of the heavens as it placed itself in waiting before her, the woman who was ready to be delivered, to devour her child. And the fire dragon, that old serpent, was he who is called the Devil, who deceiveth the whole world. And the angels shall contest him, and the child shall guide the flock with its sceptre of gold, and then be taken to heaven's throne.

THE NIGHTS AT LILLTUNA when I was a child: the insects' twitchy shadows on the nursery ceiling as they wandered across my bedside lamp. The cows lowing in the barnyard on clear moonlit nights. I sat up in my bed and called for Mam'selle Fanny, leaning against the headboard and gnawing at my nightgown until the sleeves were soaking wet, or walking around the nursery calling her name: I'd only fall silent when I heard her on the stairs, her salt-and-pepper hair tucked into her nightcap. Her narrow face would be creased with sleep and look pale in the oil-lamp light, her fingers always sooty from the kerosene as she lifted me back into bed. I'd pull a lock of hair from her cap and wind it around my finger, resting my forehead against the hollow of her throat, its beefy scent of skin and turnips and lavender. That was before she started to take her time when I called, and, when she finally did come up, would sit in the rattan armchair and send me right back if I jumped out of bed. I'd lie under the blanket, begging her to hold my hand until I fell back asleep, and over in the armchair she'd pinch her face while she drowned out my noise with readings from the Holy Scriptures. She liked especially the passages about the Beast and the signs and the trumpets and the Lamb of God: and the lake of fire burning with brimstone into which the Tempter shall be cast by a host of angels.

I begged no more, I called no more, I listened no more for her footsteps on the stairs.

Once, I went down to the hallway outside the kitchen and lay outside her door, until dawn broke and I heard her rummaging around among her things; I let my body become limp and burdensome so that despite her best efforts the door couldn't be opened, and she had to call for Krantz to carry me out of the way. The moonlight wandered across the nursery, the cows went quiet. There were times when the darkness lay smooth against my eyes like cruel velvet, and I blinked and shut them tight to keep out all the darkness beyond. Sometimes I felt as if I could cut through the night with shears, and immediately that image would fill me with dread. And the thought would come to me that, from the darkness, shapes and creatures would emerge, with edges and contours I had cut out myself, making them unstoppable, and that the cut-outs might wrap their long limbs around me like human arms, or slippery strips of pure darkness. I squeezed my eyes shut; I did not cry out for Mam'selle Fanny. Dawn would always come at last, and the sudden rim of daylight would strike the room and drive away the night. In the mornings, I'd let Fanny put me in a woollen dress and fasten the loop braids at the nape of my neck with a ribbon bow. In the evenings, I'd sit at the square piano and play for her, the hymn with the consoling name of Jesus, and the song about the young boy who burned charcoal. I no longer thought of the scent at the hollow of her neck. I sat at the nursery window and looked out at the poplars bent by the snow; I counted the fly droppings on the windowpanes as the first raw rays of sun flashed into the room and it was spring again. As soon as I heard the cabriolet arriving downstairs, I ran through the house in my white summer shoes to Doctor Eldh.

He often read to me from his works:

Albeit the uterus, since time immemorial, has been regarded as the source of various dark forms of disease, hence the innumerable manifestations of disordered nervous activity that bear the common name "hysteria"; the organ as such remains a mystery in many respects. Its influence on the rest of the organism and its pathological changes to some extent persist in defying the shrewdest investigations—

He'd sit at the walnut table under the East Indian wall clock, behind a steaming cup of chamomile tea and a plate of Mam'selle Fanny's sugar twist buns; his big face would light up or cloud over, depending on whether he was satisfied with the writing. He'd pat me on the head when our lessons came to an end or give my braid a little tug and fish a sweet from the paper bag in his waistcoat pocket. I sat opposite him and wrote in my notebooks, letting my eyes wander toward the gilded scrollwork of the clock behind him and the little pendulum inside the glass: in the middle of the dial, that black hole into infinity. Through the window, I sometimes caught glimpses of the coachmen who'd driven him to Lilltuna as they roamed between the trees at the back of the house, new men each time. There were moments when I imagined our eyes meeting through the tall windows, but outside the sun would be glaring, making it impossible for them to see me in the darkness of the room.

MY FIRST YEARS AT Lilltuna: I'd sit among the untended bushes in the English garden, eating their berries until the red juices darkened my hands and dress. I learned to walk right away. I fell, I climbed, I ran, and, so that I wouldn't disappear, I was fastened to a long rope leash that Krantz or Mam'selle Fanny were in charge of. Unpruned fruit trees grew between the small moss-covered paving stones and the archways, their burdened branches growing heavier and more gnarled. I'd climb onto the gazebo roof without a ladder, I'd watch the clouds scud and the sky break open; the leash would slide through the undergrowth behind me; I'd stick out my tongue in the pearly rain until my face ached and the big hard drops unravelled my braids. Krantz would retrieve me from the roof and remove me from the garden's nooks and crannies. In the thickest shrubberies, my leash might snag, or I'd fall asleep under the giant poplars: afterwards, I'd hold out my hands so Fanny could reprimand me, with the small cane she wore on her key belt.

Then I'd sit in the glass veranda attached to the house with a jug of hot milk and watch the evening come. Bright blue turned to red, then black. The smell of myrtle and rotting apricots wafted in from the garden. At the end of the day, I lay on the bed, eyes tracing the old damp stain above the headboard that had spread across the orchid wallpaper to make a map, while Fanny read to me on the rattan chair about the angels and the Lamb and the fire of dragons. I'd pretend to be asleep when she got up, opening the little green-painted commode and taking its contents downstairs as the brim of twilight narrowed over Lilltuna and sleep claimed me.

I discovered the first sign of my morbid disposition in the summer. When, with Mam'selle Fanny, I took my position on the front steps to greet the doctor as his carriage arrived from town, I smiled with my mouth closed so the new smell from my body wouldn't betray me. Doctor Eldh looked rosy as he stepped out of the carriage: he had so much to tell, and his arms were full of toys and a freshly tailored evening gown made of light blue half-silk for my piano recitals. He gave me a curious look as I tugged at my blouse, its sailor collar tight around my flaming neck, before going into the library and sitting down beneath the wall clock to work.

It wasn't until the evening that he called for me. He leaned back in the armchair, as was his custom, cast an appraising glance over the rims of his pince-nez, then read aloud:

With the monthly discharge, the whole uterus swells, becomes more succulent and slack in texture, though no new tissue is formed. The membrane thickens considerably, at times measuring two to three inches in diameter; it becomes loose and porous and settles into large, bulging folds. The glands, which widen and elongate, secrete mucus in profusion. There is abundant shedding of epithelial cells in the corpus uteri, which causes the membrane to lose its smooth appearance and become rough and uneven. The blood dilates and distends these vessels, with minor extravasation occurring early on, hence the outgoing mucus turns red in colour. Subsequently, the inflow of blood increases further, and vessels can rupture in great numbers, which may at times cause a significant hemorrhage: thus, the woman embodies an organism that is ever attacking itself. It is, so to speak, subject to its own invasion and must be protected and relieved accordingly by the healing arts, just as musical activity and l'esthétique relieve a darkened mind—

WHENEVER HE CAME TO visit, the doctor always brought treats from the city. Unfolding a brown paper bag he'd tucked into one of his coat pockets, he'd present shimmering pieces of amber rock sugar; on other occasions it was dried prunes or confections made of marzipan. I would hunch over my notebook, quill clamped between an index finger and a thumb sticky with the sugar, my tongue, slightly numbed by the sweetness, running imperceptibly along the backs of my rough teeth. But before this, he'd step out of the carriage with his silk top hat under his arm, as was his custom. I always greeted him on the front steps and he always beamed at the sight of me. As he reached out to stroke my hair, the bag of sweets would rustle in his coat pocket, his whiskers in clouds that billowed around his face.

He'd walk in and sit under the wall clock; he'd toss his coat over the recliner and untie his boots; he'd loosen his shirt from his vest and lean back in the chair. His papers and manuscripts and drafts were bundled thick and stored on the shelves. He came to give me my lessons; he came for a few days of uninterrupted work or to try out his remarks to the Society on me, as well as the writings he was composing for posterity. Sometimes he came only to doze on the ottoman in the library, to the sound of the blackbirds and the wind in the witch hazel outside the window. The sun would move slowly across his sleeping face. When it was time for lunch, Fanny would call us by pinging the little silver-plated dinner bell she kept on the mantelpiece in the kitchen, touched only when the doctor was visiting, and we'd be served our meal in the drawing-room. Only on those occasions was I allowed to eat in there. As soon as Doctor Eldh had returned to the city, I was ordered back to the maids' table in the kitchen with Mam'selle Fanny and Krantz and the others. But each time the doctor returned in the carriage, I was once again given my rock sugar and prompted to take my seat in the library, or to lie on the large rug to draw pictures of horses on the fragrant papers he'd supplied, after which we sat together and ate at the cracked drawing-room table. Once we had sat down, the doctor always unbuttoned his pale yellow silk vest and ran his hands through his greased mane. Then, as dusk fell outside, he served himself in silence from the pots of hen and turnip or veal shank. When he had set aside his silverware, it was my turn. To eat with him, I had to drag the screw stool from the piano to the table because the dining room set was incomplete. Lilltuna was sparsely furnished: most of what populated the rooms had been inherited from the previous owner, who, due to his imprudent lifestyle, had first had to sell off large parts of the surrounding land, and then objects and items of furniture, and finally Lilltuna in its entirety to Doctor Eldh. The East Indian wall clock was a fake and had been left behind. On the ground floor, blank squares still stood out on the wallpaper from the paintings that had been removed. Sometimes I imagined them filled with landscapes and portraits, of people I didn't know and places I'd never seen. After the doctor's visits, I always saved a piece of the shimmering amber sugar in my pinafore pocket. Once the doctor had left, I'd take it out and lick off the lint. I'd sit in the nursery window and hold it up to the sun, squinting at the tiny bubbles and irregularities behind its rusty-yellow crystal surface.

When the doctor had announced one of his impending arrivals, Fanny would run to the barn or the garden to get me so

I could wash. If we were in a hurry, I had to make do with a tub of cold water in the kitchen and Krantz trudging in and out of the entryway with buckets of water from the well. Fanny scrubbed the front of my neck and ears with a brush; she wiped the pits and folds of my face with soaked linen handkerchiefs; she placed her finger on my eyelids to wipe the dirt and grime from the corners of my eyes; she lifted my upper lip and ran the edge of one of the handkerchiefs across my teeth. I helped her with my lip so she could get in there; I lifted my chin so she could clean the pit of my neck; I soaked my hands under the water to be sure the dirt on my cuticles dissolved. Sometimes when washing me, Fanny ran the back of her hand across her cheek, as if she were wiping away an invisible tear. When Doctor Eldh was away in town, she'd always let me walk barefoot or in my wooden clogs in the pasture, though if I neglected my hands she'd reprimand me with the cane. On the occasions that the doctor's cab appeared without warning, in the distance on the crest of the hill, Fanny would dash through the garden with a fresh pair of socks and my black patent leather shoes, into which I had to stick my grubby feet, then she would tie the laces into tight knots before we ran, hand in hand, to our position on the front steps. As the cab took the curve into the courtyard, I'd sneak a glance at her other face: the face that belonged to Doctor Eldh.

On my birthdays, the doctor would read to me from the old, well-thumbed report to the Health Collegium:

Albeit I had successfully performed my first two ovariotomies during the two years prior to that point in time, and was thus not entirely unaccustomed to operating within the peritoneal cavity, I must confess: it was not without apprehension that I attempted the work of the parlous operation, which I had previously encountered only in books. The woman—a maid of delicate build and scrawny,

though flawless in bone structure excepting the malformed pelvis—
made it known that she had ever been in robust health and had
in April first felt the fetus stir. Her pulse was a steady eighty beats
per minute. How, then, to explain the protracted bleeding from the
placental site, and the gases, which defied our every effort after the
procedure and increased unceasingly until the abdomen ballooned
and its pressure led to death? I was momentarily tempted to punc-
ture a few of the distended intestinal coils, the outlines of which
could be traced across the woman's abdomen. I can only conjecture
how intestinal gases arise in such nervous states. Whence comes
the distended abdomen of the hypochondriac and the trumpeting
winds of the hysterical woman? And why do certain affections
of the mind risk being accompanied by an accumulation of gas?

Thirty hours after the incision, the patient lost consciousness,
and she expired by asphyxiation at four o'clock in the morning.
The fetus was of the female sex and fully matured: cord cut imme-
diately upon arrival and baptised statim; *apparently healthy but*
very small and delicate, much like its mother.

WHEN LITTLE BEDA CAME to Lilltuna, the man who called himself Master Valdemar had been sleeping under the East Indian wall clock for several months. He'd arrived in winter and been installed in Doctor Eldh's library, the warmest room; the doctor and Krantz had pulled him from his sleigh and helped him into the guest bed, which had been placed next to the tiled stove. The master slept behind the shut library doors; he slept through three snowstorms. Outside, Krantz and his shovel receded, deeper and deeper into the snow-covered pasture. The yellow half-light of winter days. The splayed black fingers of the trees. Spring nearing, compelled toward summer; the summer of Master Valdemar out at Lilltuna.

It took some time for Master Valdemar to notice little Beda; until he did, his thoughts were otherwise occupied. But one day, in the early summer sun, he was sipping his afternoon tea with Doctor Eldh and he discovered her. She was walking down the hill in the near distance, carrying water to the animals. The master's face was slightly haggard inside the fair curls that framed it. He stalled the raising of his cup at the sight of her.

When I was a small child, old Mam'selle Fanny and Krantz would take me down to the pond in the forest to bathe. Krantz would lift me into the wheelbarrow and then we'd parade down the uneven forest paths. This was before Hulda and Gustava entered service, back when the two black-haired sisters from Stockholm were still helping Fanny in the kitchen, and Krantz with the milking at dawn, when the day was but a shred of grey above the treetops. Both sisters had a limp, each on the opposite leg, and they looked rather alike, though one wore a blue apron and the other a brown. Sometimes they'd switch their clothes simply to confuse Fanny. At other times they'd sit under the linden trees behind the main house, cuddling and twining their hair into a single braid; later they let me touch that long black snake that writhed and flung its way across the grass. I was never told their names.

Fanny simply called the black-haired sisters "That One" and "The Other One," or "Them." Sometimes I think that had I remained in the city all those years ago, and never been taken to Lilltuna by Doctor Eldh, never been given his name and the name of the cut through which I was brought into life, I might have had a name like one of theirs. Frida or Gunn. Karlotta or Elin.

Sometimes the black-haired sisters visited my nursery at night, sneaking silently up the stairs despite their limping, so as not to wake Fanny in the housekeeper's quarters. The door gave a soft creak, and they sat down on my bed, and hushed me, and kissed the tears from my face, letting me rest my head in their laps as they stroked my hair with their sooty fingers until I fell asleep. By morning they'd be gone, but when I came down to the kitchen, there they would be again, back to normal, standing over the wheat dough or fish scraps and smiling at me, their freckled faces streaked with ash and grime.

The black-haired sisters liked to visit the pond in the forest, too; they walked alongside the wheelbarrow with their limping gaits, each with a picnic basket in hand and humming songs I didn't recognize. Wasps crawled on the bottles of elderflower cordial that stuck out of their baskets. I sat in the barrow in my walking jacket and a pale turquoise bonnet

Doctor Eldh had given me for my birthday, its strings chafing, and well into June the air would be thick with sailing white specks of aspen fluff. A yellow parasol would be lowered to shield my face from the sun. At the pond, I played with the frogs in the clear brown water that flowed between the reeds, beneath the leaves and pollen grains that made maps on the surface; I caught woodlice in a preserving jar by the rotting jetty. I climbed down the rocks and waded right into the water in my pantalettes, until my leash would tighten around my body and I'd be hauled back in. On the bank, Fanny sat under a straw hat, the leash knotted to her key belt, chewing her black tobacco. This was before she started leashing me mostly for appearance's sake, back when she still tied the rope properly to her belt. I let the pond rise to my chin and my mouth be rinsed with the fresh cold water; I floated on my back, the black-haired sisters' hands at my neck and ankles while the pantalettes ballooned around my legs. Sunlight flashing through the pines. When I came out of the water, I was wrapped immediately in the flannel blankets that had been brought along, and I'd sit shivering under the birch trees next to the sisters as they tore petals from the flowers they'd picked, rattling off the nursery rhymes they'd brought from the city. Beyond the reeds and the belt of trees opposite lay what was no longer Lilltuna: marshland and homesteads obscured by the dense forest. I could have stood up, and pulled the sunken rowboat out of the mud, and rowed right across, toward the edge of everything, and if the rowboat had sunk along the way, I'd at least have touched that border, like a brittle dying insect at the onset of winter. The black-haired sisters squinted in the bright sunlight, and giggled, and put their fingers over my eyelids and tickled my forehead with the daisies and the buttercups, though I never had a sweetheart to name in their flower games and nursery rhymes.

And it went like this with the black-haired sisters until the day they disappeared, after one trip too many to the city with Krantz to purchase groceries and supplies. In the city streets, Doctor Eldh had caught wind of their gossip, of their claims about Lilltuna and me. And when Mam'selle Fanny was called into the library, she said to the doctor, as I sat with my drawing pencils under the piano, outside the slightly open door, that she'd known it from the start: the likes of the black-haired sisters were not to be trusted. And hadn't she tried to tell the doctor so, as recently as today? Hadn't she mulled over with him her suspicions that those two had attracted other blunderers and scoundrels to the pond last summer? For Fanny did indeed think that someone had been roving around us in the woods by the bathing spot. Watching us, as it were.

After that I never made it to the pond again.

And Krantz sat alone in the cart when he returned from the city with baskets full of fruit from the market, and flour and kerosene. And the pullout sofa in the maid's room stood empty. Sometime later, Gustava and then Hulda arrived in the cab with Doctor Eldh. By then it was already winter at Lilltuna, the kind of winter that would lead to a late spring, and the heavy snow sparkled on the branches, in the golden haze that pierced through the blanket of sky at midday, only to withdraw in the dark of afternoon.

Every now and then, I thought of the clear brown water down at the pond that summer, of the water spiders jumping on the surface, and the cool sweetness I filtered into my mouth, and the lightness of my body below that surface, and the woodlice that were thrown away. When the next summer arrived, I would sit on the veranda with the doctor's early-reader books while, on the bench below, Gustava worked the dasher in the butter churn, and Krantz returned with his fishing rod and wet trouser hems and two bunches of young pike hanging at his belt. I didn't ask about the pond: I never went further than the edge of the garden. I no longer thought about what lay beyond Lilltuna. Out there, the wattle fences cleaved the landscape up, and the wood pigeons soared above the marshes, and, at the long table at supper, I sat between Fanny and Hulda, eating turnips and egg soup and the fried fish Krantz had pulled from the brown water, mashing the pale salty flesh against the roof of my mouth. I could have walked through the garden, my leash trailing behind me in the grass, and taken the shortcut across the meadow down to the pond, and waded to the other side. I could have run across the fields, straight onto the main road, shouting to attract the attention of the hay carts and the crowds of children I sometimes saw playing outside the farms in the distance. The tangled wall of bird cherry and hawthorn that framed Doctor Eldh's property was never pruned. As time went by, since she'd noticed that I never stole away, Fanny let me play longer and longer in the garden or behind the barn, where I'd sit with the dolls and the carved wooden horse Doctor Eldh had given me for my birthday. The leash would be slack around my waist and muddied by the sodden ground. Hours could pass before Fanny would ask Krantz to bring me back in, and she knew I'd always return by dark.

I WONDERED FOR A long time why Doctor Eldh continued to keep me at Lilltuna, why I was kept away from the hay carts passing in the distance and the children playing on the wattle fences: I no longer wonder. Daddy-long-legs swaying over the lamp's green glass. The steely eye of the East Indian wall clock facing its own eternity. I had brown hair; I had open palms; I sat in the red, the yellow, the forest-green woollen dresses and played the piano in the evenings, or I was leashed in the garden's unclipped green grass. Above Lilltuna the sun wandered, colouring the house purple and gold. Swarms of gnats above the animals in the pasture.

Sometimes the doctor was already in a temper when he arrived in the cab, and on the front steps he'd give my head a hasty and indifferent pat before going inside. I'd press my ear to the library door, listening to him unlock the wall clock as he always did: he'd open the little window to the clock face and then shut it with a snap. I often imagined that time itself began there, in the doctor's library, at the very moments when he spun the hands around the dial and set the clock in motion: that each of his absences made time retreat, and that during that time I'd be back in the garden under the trees, among the dolls that had been played to pieces, everything extended into one long moment.

Sometimes Doctor Eldh seemed irritated during my lessons; sometimes he would stare out the window for a long time and I would scribble aimlessly in my notebook so as not to attract his attention, though the sound of the nib scratching against the paper filled the room. Then he might fly from his chair and start pacing back and forth across the rug, impatient or absent-minded, talking and shaking his fist in the air as if arguing with someone only he could see. *The damned upstart,* he might exclaim. *Imagine drawing that conclusion!* Or: *The sycophant thinks he knows a thing or two about uterine prolapse!* And, once in a while, a simple: *Bastard!*

I'd sit in the undergrowth in the garden, licking my arms to taste my body's salt; I'd bite down on my fingers and watch the grooves made by my teeth darken: I didn't bring bodies into connection. I would wait for Doctor Eldh, and when he returned I would read his face and gestures like one studies an unruly current. He often tested out his writings on me there at the walnut table, regularly glancing up from the page while reading aloud to observe my reactions, and, when he did, I'd always beam. Then, from behind his pince-nez, a glow of satisfaction would come, and he'd proceed:

Of the Caesarean section, we can state, without risk of exaggeration, that since Trautmann performed the first scientifically recorded sectio caesarea *in 1610, it has been performed at least two thousand times. On each occasion, a representative of our profession found that a fetus could not be brought forth, either alive or else dead and in pieces,* per vias naturales, *and thus was emboldened to reach for the scalpel. Upon my first case of incision, during which I found the fetus wedged in the upper left corner of the maternal cavity, as if in a sack and robbed of sight, it was instinct rather than deliberation that enabled me to place my hand underneath the abdomen of the fetus at the critical juncture, and to force its back through the cut, whereupon it exited the womb doubled over, the child's life saved in the same breath it lost its mother. In our vocation, we witness life's burdens as well as its miracles: I'd dare to say that the Caesarean section's virgin-birth-in-reverse is not among the lesser of such miracles. Thus, the fortunate surgeon himself becomes the author of the human delivery* per excellentiam, *hitherto reserved for woman.*

As far back as I can remember, I remember sitting in the library, listening to Doctor Eldh read aloud his drafts and remarks for Society meetings, after which he'd smile gratefully as if relieved of a burden unknown to me. Sometimes he'd burst into tears and bury his face in the crook of his arm, at which point I knew he wanted me to reach across the table and lay my hand on his mighty skull. *Forgive me, Kitten,* he might murmur into the sleeve of his shirt. *Say you forgive me.*

Sometimes when the crying stopped, he'd look up at me with his red-rimmed eyes and say my name. His eyelashes would be limp with tears and his cheeks as pink and blotchy as a small child's. After he'd wiped his face, he would once more tell the story of my Creation, how he had saved me from the road to perdition and had given me a name. He'd say that I reminded him of something but he couldn't think of what. A taste on his tongue. Thunderstorms from his childhood. The scents of wood and skin in the bed he shared with his siblings in the summertime. The animals' strange sounds as they moved through the forest outside his childhood home. He stressed repeatedly that they had beckoned him.

I lay my hand on his head, as he wished, and asked: *How are children tucked into bed at night out there in the city, Doctor Eldh?*

He looked at me with those tearful eyes and answered: *They are tucked into the darkness of the world, child, into its wretched cold.*

THE FIRST SYMPTOM OF my morbid disposition was a boil on my right-hand side: I discovered it in the summer, after a Saturday bath. The gaps in the sky, the troubled clouds at night. In the dark, the garden trees looked like burnt fingers. I was still a child. I had learned to fall asleep to the scratch of rowan branches against my window; I lay in bed as the seasons came and went. Sometimes I counted the cracks and creaks that moved through the house, which seemed to expand and draw nearer in the dark, as if every sound out at Lilltuna might at last flock around me and become a clarifying light inside my dreams, or radiant images I could never remember when I woke up. When I couldn't sleep, I would sit at the nursery window and look out over the pasture. Down there, the slow shadows of the grazing animals floated on the grassy hills, black formations crowding and spreading across the shimmering pale grey ground.

I stood with a sheet wrapped around my body and inspected myself, my braids dripping down my back. The symptom had appeared just above my ribs, on my front: a pink stain with a small wart in the centre that had suddenly begun to protrude. It now resembled a small swollen plum, emerging from the previously smooth and faintly flesh-coloured area, a boil rising like dough and wrenching its way out of the skin, as if the body could no longer contain itself: its rosy centre was like a blunt and nasty bite. Only my right side was affected, giving a distorted and asymmetrical impression.

I walked around with the boil for a long time, dressing

and eating Fanny's oat soup and doing what I was supposed to while keeping quiet about my symptom: then it began on the other side. This other boil was worse than the former, so I began to bandage them both. A similar course of growth, uneven at first, followed in other places. I lay in bed and sensed the new smell of fish guts coming from the slit between my legs, with its variably shaped flaps of skin now sticking out between the mounds on each side, those slightly downy hills, soft as a newborn animal. The high-summer night sky and the unfamiliar smell kept me awake. Then the bleeding began.

I stopped washing so as not to chafe the infected areas with the scrub brush; I let the slit clot up; I noticed redness on my neck and forehead and further swelling; I bandaged my chest; I waited for it to recede; I stank of month-old sweat and the slit's musty serum; my arms grew pale as if the boils were drawing the life out of them. Fanny stood on the glass veranda, following me with her eyes as I strolled under the trees in the garden. I felt moisture press out of my armpits and my face flare up at the slightest excitement; it was the body's expulsion of itself. It pushed itself out of me as I sat with my game of solitaire next to Fanny and her embroidery, or practised scales on the piano. In the evenings, I threw the stained pantalettes into the commode because I didn't know what else to do with them; when I woke up, the commode would be empty, returned and clean in its usual place. By the tub in the kitchen where Fanny had begun to leave me alone to wash, I gave the water a vigorous stir but didn't get in; I only dipped my hair and rinsed my face. Afterwards, I wrapped a sheet around my unwashed body and went to the door, my hair's wet tendrils tossed over my shoulders; each time Fanny stood there outside, waiting for me with that penetrating gaze. She held out the little cotton rags that she folded and pressed and sewed ties onto, and I went upstairs and put them inside my clothes between my thighs, knotting the ties snugly around my hips.

I braided my hair myself; I pressed the air out of my body and tightened the bandages around the boils.

I did not yet have the Sceptre I acquired that final summer, to vanquish the Beast with breath Burning from each of its seven Heads.

I clothed myself in the freshly laundered pantalettes laid out for me on the bed; I didn't touch the slit's swollen flaps protruding from the swirls of down; I beat the sick body back into its hollows. I waited for Doctor Eldh, for him to come back and cure me.

IN MY NINTH YEAR, the doctor started training me to take dictation. We sat as usual in the library, the walnut table cleared but for writing instruments and blank paper. From the sideboard, the portraits of his daughters stared at me through the small glass ovals: above, the black eye of the wall clock. I learned penmanship; I learned to spell; the doctor let me use the black steel pen and the finest ink. I clamped the pen between my index finger and thumb, refining my handwriting by imitating Doctor Eldh's scrolling letters until they were indistinguishable from my own; when the ink dripped, I was quick with the blotting paper.

Doctor Eldh always spoke from memory, walking between the half-empty bookshelves and lecturing straight into the air to no one in particular. When he fell silent and became pensive, I leaned the tip of my pen against the well and let it drip while I waited, watching his face: the fine lines, the trustful expression, the meditative creases of his forehead. I almost could have walked up to him where he stood looking for the words and rested my forehead against his waistcoat-clad chest. Sometimes I became sleepy from waiting and started fumbling with the writing instruments and blotting paper; sometimes I spilled the ink across the table's shiny surface. Then he'd turn around with a disappointed expression and ask me to begin again. Outside, the poplars towered, their unnaturally tall trunks beneath the brittle grey afternoon skies. Now and again Krantz would look at us through the window as he and the chestnut horse passed by, or when he was about to show one of the drivers the guest bed in the farmhand's cottage: his eyes always looked strange and unseeing, and I realized that the black mirror of the window's glass made me invisible.

On a few occasions, the doctor took his scrawny one's pubic bone out of the desk drawer and held it up in the afternoon light so I could study its curvature. Once, he let me touch it gently with my index finger: the grey-white surface was polished clean and shiny, like oiled leather that had been handled for a long time. In his report to the Health Collegium, he had written, under a small charcoal line drawing:

> *In its overall character, the object shows a relatively constricted female pelvis with no notable anomaly in texture. The following deviations can be observed: the lateral walls run a straighter course than usual and find union in the pubic symphyses at a more acute angle than is the norm; the sacrum presents the most significant deviation both in form and position; the width between the two sacroiliac joints is normal, but they are compressed from above and below, so that the anterior surface forms an almost complete semicircle, on either side of which the corners form, sharply receding, wide and deep bays—*

There were times when I felt ill at ease during my lessons or when walking alone in the garden: behind my eyes there'd be a swirl of something indescribable, something brewing, and I would cover my eyelids with my fingers to still the movement. Afterwards, I'd spit in my palms and smooth my hair, from my part down to the root of my braid. Fanny never failed to make a perfectly straight part in my hair. She'd put the comb to my scalp and split the swell of hair with a single stroke, the furrow of scalp flashing red afterwards. Every so often, after the doctor had travelled back to the city, she would cry in the housekeeper's quarters, a strange sob that left her eyes swollen the next day; I never knew what she was crying about. And Doctor Eldh always came back. As soon as the carriage approached, she'd grab hold of me and scrub me with the rag, or come running out to me with the patent leather shoes. When we stood on the front steps, her hands cupping my shoulders, she'd already put on that face she wore when the doctor arrived. It smiled and squinted: beneath it lay the dry, strange fear of the original.

Afterwards, I sat at the walnut table again and wrote while Doctor Eldh dictated; I got faster and faster and performed my task with increasing skill. Sometimes I thought intensely of the doctor's touch as I sat there with the pen, writing away; I thought of it as of the crumbs one licks from a table after someone else's meal. The doctor never touched me, other than the small appreciative tugs of my braid at the end of dictation practice or the light pats on my head on the stairs when he arrived, and sometimes our fingers would meet for a moment as he slipped me a treat from the brown paper bag. The only times he took hold of me were for my annual checkups, which he performed with Mam'selle Fanny's assistance: then, his big hands searched my body, holding and squeezing my limbs to inspect my growth, tickling me on the soles of my feet to check my reflexes, and sticking the silver instruments into my mouth to study my throat while Fanny stood by in case I made a fuss. I never did; I perched on the desk and allowed myself to be inspected. Doctor Eldh's hands were warm and almost inhumanly dry. I gaped at the instruments; I lifted my skirt and bunched my pantalettes up around my thighs so he could knock on my kneecaps with the little wooden yellow-stained hammer.

FIRST I GOT THE black-haired sisters, then little Beda.

In my memory, I see her turning around in the carriage on the crest of the hill, in a final farewell: that was after we'd been retrieved from the pond and they came to drive her away. The white oval of her face, inside the tightly knotted shawl, as her carriage rounded the crest, then vanished.

After the black-haired sisters were taken from me, I would sit in the barnyard, on top of the overturned wheelbarrow that leaned against the wall, chewing on a blade of grass and watching Krantz and Mam'selle Fanny while they looked after the animals. That wasn't Fanny's responsibility, but after the black-haired sisters were sent away and we awaited new helpers, there was no one else in the house to help with the milking. Sometimes Fanny's and Krantz's movements in the courtyard woke me at dawn and I'd run downstairs, my sheepskin coat pulled over my plain-weave linen, so I could watch. Mam'selle Fanny would let me, as she clasped her hands around the big spotted teats and tugged. The pissing sound when the milk hit the enamel. The cows' udders were always fit to burst at that hour, and the cows lowed at us when we came into the stalls, though Fanny never hurried for their sake. Krantz used to hand me a little wooden cup to drink from, which he'd dipped into the steaming buckets. The warm yellow liquid settled on my palate and tongue with a slippery, tickling coating. I sat on the overturned wheelbarrow, the blade of grass growing slippery with milk residue in my mouth, and dozed off while Krantz and Fanny did their rounds in the stalls. That was before Hulda and Gustava came out to Lilltuna and started helping Krantz with the cows so Fanny didn't have to. After they arrived, I was no longer allowed down there at daybreak, though I tried a few times, running down the stairs in my sheepskin. Fanny would be there at the foot of the stairs, ready with a look that told me to turn right back around. I'd lie back in bed and listen to Krantz and Hulda and Gustava, their steps creaking in the snow, and Hulda's low, incessant, warbling voice before the barn door shut behind them: she had the irksome song of a flighty bird. I thought of the black-haired sisters, of their nursery rhymes and their single snake of hair and their hands at my nape down by the pond. I sat on the pile of wood in the kitchen, gnawing on crusts of old bread and scowling at Hulda and Gustava while they joked around, stirring the kettle or unpacking the eggs from the basket, the small, damp-slick feathers sticking to their aprons and hands, though as soon as Mam'selle Fanny appeared in the doorway, her cane creaking on her belt, they'd fall silent. There in the kitchen, Hulda was always whispering silly little stories in Gustava's ear with her wide red mouth. Her birdlike breathing made Gustava's pocked face blush in an ugly way under her cap, but Hulda continued her warbling and flirting and let that wide mouth open and close around her secrets. That was before I had begun to lurk around the house, my body Bound so it would keep itself inside its cavities, and before the time I caught them, by chance, when they thought no one was watching, out in the garden, on the hill where they had been sent to pick raspberries for the late summer jam.

I didn't make myself known. Instead, I crouched behind the bird cherry and allowed them their imagined solitude. Hulda was carrying on as usual there among the raspberries, whispering her tittle-tattle in Gustava's ear, and Gustava blushed as always under her cap. But then, suddenly, Hulda fell silent, staring at Gustava with that broad grin stretched across her face before grabbing both of Gustava's hands, pulling them toward her and pressing them to her body. Gustava let out a soft groan, and her hands began to fidget with and grope at the flesh bulging under Hulda's clothes, and with this Hulda began her warbling again. She began to coo like a bird and preen herself, and exhaled her hot breath on Gustava's neck, and Gustava searched and groped her flesh, and let herself be enticed. And one, two, three, Hulda had unbuttoned her blouse, and inside were the two little lumps, quivering and tempting in the sparks of sunshine falling through the canopy of leaves overhead. They weren't like the swollen boils I bandaged in the evenings: Hulda's winter-white skin curved softly underneath the fresh, strawberry-red roundels with their stiff, slightly darker peaks. Gustava whimpered and seemed to waver on her feet, her hands around Hulda's waist as if she had drunk the wine in Doctor Eldh's cabinet or were walking in her sleep. But Hulda just held the lumps out toward Gustava in the light, and talked and coaxed with that voice, and then she cupped Gustava's cheeks and pressed her face to the gap in her blouse. And all the while she was talking her bird talk, and her wide mouth was in its grin, teasing and babbling while she let her lumps be rubbed. And suddenly she pulled her skirts up over her belly and exposed herself to Gustava, who again groaned, salivated, and fell to her knees in the raspberries: and so Gustava sat for a while, her fingers like a sleepwalker's, tripping along Hulda's folds and hollows. The pink slit gleamed between Hulda's legs like a strip of uncooked pig flesh slung between her tufts of brown hair. Then, all at once, Hulda ceased her stirring and talking, and fell silent and shut her eyes, and let her head drop back against a tree trunk, and the only sound was Gustava's groaning next to the wound between Hulda's legs, and the low clucking of the wound being made to weep by Gustava's hands. Until Hulda suddenly opened her eyes again, and gave a shudder, and let her gaze flit for a few moments, and scud strangely across the trees, and then of a sudden she dropped her skirts. And pulled away, and closed her blouse. And buttoned all the buttons, all the way up to the collar. She smiled her bird smile again as she picked up the bucket that lay toppled on the ground before disappearing among the raspberries.

Gustava stayed on the hill, her spent face and hands gleaming with the moisture from Hulda's wound. She was no longer moaning. Then she pulled her cap off, leaving her braids tousled at the nape, and mopped up the moisture with it until her face looked ugly, red and mottled. Then I stood up behind the bird cherry and retreated into the thicket. Patches of sun darted through the greening canopy and sailed and careened across my clothing.

In the evening I lay in the nursery, listening to the tawny owl. I didn't think about what had happened among the raspberries, I slept with the bandage tight around my chest, I yawned in the darkness as if I could fill my mouth with the image of those ruddy lumps. In my dreams they were salty and pleasant, deceptively soft, like old, spoiled fruit. I awoke at dawn to footsteps on the gravel courtyard below, and the sound of tittle-tattle, then the barn door being opened and shut.

THE FIRST THING I learned was Lilltuna, and Lilltuna was Doctor Eldh's. He came and went back to his daughters in the city, though always returning after a few weeks: only once did it take longer, and that was when he went away on a long tour of the continent. Then, he left in early summer and didn't come back until Lilltuna was a-whirl with snow. Upon his return, he wasn't alone: the master was with him. Who, staggering and supported on both sides, stepped out of the covered sleigh that winter evening, his coat dotted with large white snowflakes.

The strained light of those brief January days. A lost fox skidding across the night-frosted yard.

Before saying goodbye and leaving on the long tour, the doctor came out to Lilltuna one last time to give me my lessons. Early June. He was excited; his mutton chops were groomed and his mane of hair greased with pomade, making him look like a gentle, gleaming lion about to go out on the prowl. He sat in the library with the bottom of his dickie sticking out of his waistcoat like a bib, his luggage open around him. During my lessons, he was absent-minded, occasionally feeding me rock sugar. He carefully placed his documents and inkwells in their little compartments and boxes in the trays of his luggage trunks, and explained that he thought he might be away until just before Christmas. He travelled the next day. He did not return until well into the new year.

The angled early-summer sunlight sparkling and streaming through the branches of the witch hazel. July came, then August. In the doctor's absence, I ran barefoot through the garden, I lay on my belly on the kitchen stairs and split ants with my thumbnail.

That summer I often sat by the hawthorn hedge that grew around Lilltuna, playing with the tin soldiers and the small porcelain princess given to me by Doctor Eldh and building castles out of cones and twigs. I ate the wood sorrel and chewed the wall fern's roots and, with fingertips dipped in the wet earth, I painted letters and animals on my thighs and arms. Sometimes I listened to the passing carts; sometimes they came so close I could hear the chafing of a draft animal's headstall against its bit. Shrill children's voices. Running my fingers over the hawthorn's dense foliage, I always returned to the house before nightfall. The sweep of twilight above Lilltuna was flecked with cloud.

It always happened after bedtime, when the darkness grew dense and Fanny had gone downstairs: the image of the shears returned in the night, and the darkness again became pitch-black velvet that could be cut and turned into strange things and creatures. And the cut-out creatures emerged from the night shadows and wrapped themselves around me with their strips or fingers, and the only remedy was to repeat Fanny's stories about the Lord Jesus as best I could remember. The creatures moved around me without a sound. They were as silent as the darkness from which they had come, with their alien, absent faces without mouths or eyes. They seemed to want something from me, I didn't know what, though it was me who'd clipped them out of the darkness like paper dolls. I lay in bed and recited the words about the thunder of horns and the Staff of the Anointed that would drive away the Beast, then it eased a bit and I managed to fall asleep. But in my sleep came dreams that began bright and watery, and a lake appeared that resembled the bathing pond in the forest on that hot summer's day. And an image floated up of the black-haired sisters, and all at once they were stood over on the far side of the pond, each raising a hand and waving a little at me, as if to reassure me or to signal that if I would only cross the brown water, they'd be waiting for me. Then suddenly the picture changed, and I no longer knew if I was dreaming or awake, and the pond transformed and glowed and sizzled and spilled its banks like molten lava, a liquid fire, and I realized that they'd lured me into a trap, and the monster that must be cast into the lake of fire was none other than myself. I heard a cracking inside my head and I opened my eyes, forcing myself out of the drowsiness that resembled neither sleep nor waking, the smell of Fanny's morning gruel on the stove downstairs rising through the tiles.

August went.

September came.

Autumns at Lilltuna brought with them the smell of dead badgers and fallen fruit. I walked barefoot in the needles under the spruces, my feet no longer feeling their pricks after my shoeless summer, I let the ants crawl over my calves. I waited for Doctor Eldh, for him to come back and cure me. I received a letter stamped from the continent:

5 October

My heart!

We arrived at the hospital on Rue Jacob on a balmy evening, where Dr. Beaufeu received us with open arms, and we were led into the gynecological operating theatre where the many suffering creatures now flock daily to place their lives in the hands of the venerable surgeon. This horde of unfortunate souls is seeking cures for all manner of ailments related to the female sexual system: masturbation, nymphomania, ovarian inflammation, retroflexion of the uterus, et cetera. Remarkably, here on the continent these common afflictions of the lower abdomen have been freed from their secrecy, and many are they who seek treatment in the modern hospitals, where scissors and scalpel, probe, ring, mirror, and pin are presented to them by eminent doctors—with which they are to be examined, burned, corroded, and cut, and their cysts, lumps, and tumours extirpated. At eight o'clock the theatre curtain was drawn back, and a young lady in a fit of nervous sobs, whose fitful breathing allowed Dr. Beaufeu's hand to penetrate deeply and without resistance, was first thoroughly examined, and then sent to sleep with ether. We then witnessed from the best vantage point the most perfect ovarian incision any in our travelling party had ever before seen.

In the mornings I am awakened by the children playing outside the hotel; I enjoy my morning tea on a small balcony under which a rich street life jostles with hurrying cabs, tireless shopping in boutiques, and gentlemen and ladies having breakfast outside the bakeries. The trees are very beautiful and unusual here, stretching their branches ever closer to the sky as their dense crowns slowly rustle in the breeze. The flecks of light darting around the wall above my bed remind me of my diligent little rascal out at Lilltuna. Well: how does my little girl fare? Be kind to Fanny and the others.
Faithful greetings, Dr. E

THE SKY WAS THIN and yellow, unreal. Last year's grass, bared in a thaw. The bright sun burned the tops of my hands as I played in the garden. Then more snow. Skies that swelled and thinned as when you stream water through milk.

At that time, I always wore the white pinafore or sailor costume to Doctor Eldh's lessons in the library. And after the lessons, I went up to my nursery and exchanged these simpler outfits for the more expensive evening pieces the doctor had had made for me in the cities he'd visited on his travels. Once dressed, I went downstairs in the twilight and sat on the stool at the piano and waited for the doctor and Fanny to make themselves comfortable on the blue drawing-room sofa behind me. I found my anchor point in the little nail hole in the centre of the faded square on the wall above the lid of the piano; by way of introduction I marked the silence by resting my fingers lightly on the keys, and then I played. The grinding of the instrument's invisible mechanics reached me from its bowels, the tension of the strings, the creaking of the sounding board. The piano was old and damaged by damp due to its prior owner's neglect, and at times the notes sounded so wavering or off-key that the doctor had to get up from the sofa and come over and place his hand over my fingers to prevent me from playing any further. On his next visit he brought along from the city the man who tuned pianos.

The piano tuner, unlike the coachmen, was always the same little man and wore the same dark blue overcoat. When he tested the notes, the sounds reached all the way through the house to my nursery: they were by turns impatient and pensive. I imagined him running his finger along the pins and the cracks in the keys, or feeling to make sure the felt cushions were still in place on the small hammers: then came the clinking of the company porcelain left behind by Lilltuna's previous owner, as the tuner, his work complete, was invited to elderberry tea in the drawing-room with Doctor Eldh.

When he had visited often enough to hold a position of trust, I was also invited to tea with the piano tuner, and the doctor would ask me to play a happy melody. I played marches and ballads and sonatas; Doctor Eldh sometimes sat next to me and we'd play with four hands. When I turned around, the tuner would always be on the sofa, applauding; he had small, gnarled hands with a black-rimmed nail on each finger, and his eyes shone as if he were regarding an exotic animal. He always gave me the same look during his visits, and on occasion, when the cab was driven up for the piano tuner to part, the doctor would allow him to take my hand and I would curtsy deep and long. I noticed that the doctor disliked it when the tuner stared at me for too long during the piano sessions; then, he'd ask me to go to my room, and I wouldn't be allowed to come out to say farewell on the front steps, and it would be a long time before the tuner came back to Lilltuna. But when the square piano began to rattle too much and the notes became too wobbly, the doctor would relent and summon him again.

The tuner brought me small gifts: a blue box with a fake pearl bracelet; a small mechanical dog with soft, curly grey fur that could be wound up with a tiny key and made to walk a few steps across the table before it fell off, onto its back on the drawing-room rug. There it would lie for a while, fumbling the air like a helpless spider, whereupon the tuner would pick it up with his black-rimmed fingers and wind it up again. Now and then, invisible moods and dramas passed between the little man in the dark blue coat and the doctor, sheer clouds thrashing in the air. But in the end, the tuner was always forgiven for whatever it was he'd done to anger Doctor Eldh, and soon the cab from the city would return again, and the tuner would step out onto the courtyard in front of the house with his small glossy trunk filled with tuning apparatuses. When he arrived, depending on the doctor's spirits, I was allowed to sit at the piano and play, the tuner behind me on the sofa, unless I was shown back to my room or instructed to sit with the doctor in the library with the door shut while the tuner was present in the house. Then I would fix the black steel pen between the fingers of one hand and grasp the paper with the other, and Doctor Eldh would begin his dictation.

It was Fanny who taught me the piano. She used to say that in a previous life she had acquired the gift of music; otherwise, she told me very little about what she'd done and where she'd been before she became the mam'selle of Lilltuna and responsible for my care. Mostly she played hymns and songs of praise, and I followed her fingers across the instrument as one listens for the unpredictable sound of the cuckoo before the trees come into leaf. Sometimes, at dawn, she might go with Krantz to make purchases in the city, hoping to find new sheet music for me; she always made sure I was properly guarded by Hulda and Gustava. They got into the habit, once she'd gone, of leashing me and then nagging me to play pony behind the linden trees; to stop their nagging, I might run a lap between the trunks if they gave me something valuable in exchange: a hairpin or a shell or some other trinket they kept in the overstuffed luggage they'd brought from the cities and villages I knew nothing of. Then Hulda would laugh with her big shiny face, Gustava echoing her. When I had run my lap, I'd sit with my back to the two of them, under the furthest linden tree, the rope still tied around my waist as I devoted myself to my traded goods. They'd sit on the kitchen stairs, peeling turnips or plucking chickens, with my rope tied to a hook in the wall, though they knew I'd never wander off anyway. They might entertain themselves by playing with the cat when she was in heat and would writhe against the corners of the house; once, they grabbed her by the hind legs while wearing Krantz's winter gloves as she thrashed and scratched and yowled, until the feral toms gathered and lined up at the edge of the forest to call to her, and then they released her. Her cries in the forest went on for hours while the tomcats had their way with her beneath the trees.

There were times when Hulda and Gustava became so bored there on the kitchen stairs that they fell asleep; I easily could have loosened the rope and walked straight out into the garden and further, across the fields and the hilly pasture beyond Lilltuna. While they dozed, I leaned my back against the trunk of the linden tree, I scratched the hairpin along my nail beds or put the curved shell to my ear, I did not loosen the leash.

When the cart returned at dusk, Fanny, if she'd had any success in the city, had with her the cheap sheet music she'd bought somewhere, and we'd spend the next few days practising at the piano. Outside, the trees in the garden bowed with the fruit Krantz hadn't had time to pick. Fanny dragged the armchair next to the screw stool; she hovered her hands above the keys and marked the silence, then let her fingers run and her face focus inward as she unleashed the music from the instrument. When it was my turn to play, and I wasn't concentrating properly on reading the notes, she might rap her knuckles impatiently on the lid. I'd let my fingertips tap the cracked surfaces of the keys, listening for Fanny's knocks and sighs and hums at each misstep or note hit, adjusting my emphasis and speed according to her reactions. There were times when I pretended to misread the music and would have to start again. Then she'd land her knuckle on the piano lid and lean forward, at times coming so close that I could sense her coarse tobacco breath on my neck and the faint scent of her skin. Every time I lost my thread or couldn't hold the tone, she'd punish me by slapping my fingers with the sheet music a few times, after which I always played with a clarity that felt blessed. Through the clinking, I could hear Fanny's low smack of satisfaction as the music swelled.

DOCTOR ELDH TOOK ME into his care and kept me at Lilltuna as one preserves a pearl; perhaps he kept me simply because he could. He left but he came back: to drive me around the countryside in the cab for fresh air; to make sure I did not remain ignorant of the names of countries, trees, and constellations, or of the arts of calligraphy and arithmetic; he came so that I would lay my hand upon that big head of his across the table while he cried. Late summers, turning and fading and moving toward autumn. The clear September air in and out of the lungs. The scent of pine. The thrushes flocking to the rowan outside my window. In the evenings, I would lie in bed and listen to Mam'selle Fanny rummaging about in the chamber downstairs before she went to bed, the low murmur of her evening prayers rising through the house. Minor streaks of impending cold. In the night, at the tree line, foxes called, and at dawn, the first unrestrained sunlight flowed into my room: the toys would already be covered, and I'd turned the dollhouse to face the wall. I practised writing quickly at the desk; I played hopscotch around the back though I'd long since outgrown the game. In the garden, Krantz moved with the hedge shears between the poplars or walked the furrowed fields, shaking the potato tubers from their stems.

The chestnut horse that grew old, the piebald that was bought for the new carriage.

I lay on my back on the roof of the gazebo, I waited for rain; I was always the most afraid of empty skies. I liked to count the cumulus clouds as they floated by, rending to pieces the infinite blue. I liked the rain; I always let it whip down onto my dresses and the wetness seep into my skin. Sometimes smoke would rise from the small fires Krantz built in the pasture to give the animals relief from the gnats, pillars of grey shooting into the sky before dissipating. I sat on the red-painted pasture gate while Krantz stabled the cows for the night, following the smoke with my eyes, straight up into nothing.

At the cusp of autumn, I went with Krantz and Hulda and Gustava to pick peat moss in the forest for the cattle and then bale it for the winterfeed; the finest hay was saved for the young bulls that Krantz collected from the farms further away so they could mount the cows in late spring. Krantz had me by the leash when we went foraging in the forest: we wove our way between the piles of rock and the anthills and the fallen trunks, and, should we meet someone out there on the paths, he had instructed me to withdraw between the trees. A short time into winter he'd let me sit on the bench in the barn and watch as Hulda and Gustava fed the cows the cooked moss they'd mixed with leaves and horse manure, though we gave none of the moss to the lambs and pigs. December was a feeble grey light along the field's horizon. Krantz would sit next to me on the bench, wearing the thick coat he'd padded with hay, consumed with smearing the halters with goat butter while the cows munched through their feed. Afterwards, he'd look up at me in a daze through the clouds made by his breath; my lips would be stiff with cold, and he'd throw off his coat and wrap it around me.

I was never allowed to attend the mating in the spring: I'd be put in the nursery, the door locked from the outside. When mating season arrived in the year I was to turn ten, Gustava talked at supper about how a farm boy had once been pinned to a barn wall by a young bull that had come loose on the farm where she used to work, and how the boy's parents and the farmer had not dared to approach for several hours because the bull was goring and rending to pieces anything it could reach. And the bull couldn't be reined in: he trampled and trod on the boy out in the yard as if the child were simply a rag, pushing the body around as the intestines spilled from the gut. And they tried and failed to catch the bull in their sights, until finally someone hit the mark. But by then the boy was as good as cut in two and had been dead for hours.

I was locked inside the nursery; I sat at the window and watched the little dot on the road get bigger and divide into three: the neighbouring farmer, Krantz, and the bull.

I was the most afraid of cloudless skies. I sat in my sailor's costume at the walnut table while Doctor Eldh dictated. I wrote:

> *Memories and notes of service. When I, as a recently graduated doctor, served for a time in Malmö, a memorable case fell to my lot. A woman had been thrown from a pony at a fairground attraction in one of the city's parks, after a mutt's barking had caused the creature to bolt. The woman fell briskly from the frightened animal and landed on the ground with the full, not-inconsiderable weight of her body straight upon her pelvis. I examined her later, at her home, where she was at rest on a bolstered bed that had been arranged by the servants and a choleric husband. The patient complained of pain in the lower back, pelvis, and even the rectum, and I understood at once what it might be: if there was one thing I despised at that time, it was the examination of female genitalia. I plucked up the courage and palpated the abdomen and lower back, after which retroflexion of the uterus due to the unfortunate fall could be determined. I then remembered a piece of advice I'd received as a medical student from an older mentor regarding a dislocated uterus: the*

advice was to place the patient on her elbows and knees, and then introduce one finger into the rectum and another into the vagina, and then, with all one's might and repeatedly, one was to press upward and downward. "If that measure does not make the whole thing fall into place, then surely nothing else will!" my mentor had said to me. I asked the woman to assume the position, and I inserted fingers one and two into the patient's cavities. I could immediately feel the womb and began to push. Suddenly, I felt nothing more than a cavity, as if I had put my fingers in a hat and was moving them around inside it, encountering neither lining nor crown. The woman then looked over her shoulder at me and exclaimed: "Dear doctor, I am relieved!" As I pulled my hand out of her, there was a loud explosion, after which the mortified woman apologized profusely, especially as the burst of air had not come from the bowel. The insight was strange: how air could penetrate the female body and force an entire organ to tilt back. And there was also the sensation I had that her body was a mighty instrument, in which my fingers could be driven in one direction or another, and a surprising music could emerge from its chambers. On my way back to the servants' quarters, an ice-green daylight shimmered above the city, and I had overcome my juvenile fear of female genitalia—

Silver skies. The evenings before the mating seasons began, I'd follow Krantz and Hulda and Gustava out to the barnyard, watching them go into the stalls and draw crosses of tar on the cows' rumps so the bulls wouldn't be too rough with them. The tar was supposed to make the cows smell worse and the bulls less eager. Krantz had agreements with several of the farms around Lilltuna: usually, young bulls born in the spring that the farmer had fattened over the winter were invited to mate. In the autumn, the yearlings were slaughtered and we'd buy the meat for Christmas. One year, I was given a piece of a bull's ear to play with. The ear was light brown and smooth and calf-like, I put it in the ruby-rose box among the pine cones I'd collected in the garden. If Doctor Eldh's cows calved bulls, they'd be sold to a nearby farm: Krantz did not want to tend to any wild beasts, he'd say, on top of everything else that needed tending to at Lilltuna. The bull calves were picked up early and taken away in carts on their unsteady legs: afterwards, the cow that had lost her calf would cry for a long time at the pasture gate. Sometimes the cows got tricky after they'd calved, especially if they'd been heifers during the mating season, and had not been kept inside during the calving but had gone off and calved in solitude: those cows went feral, and wouldn't let anyone near, and were intractable and kept their newborns away from Krantz in the pasture, and Krantz would have to spend a long time in there coaxing them so he could get hold of the calves. But, in the end, he always prevailed, and would take the calf away, and for days the cow would trot around the pasture, searching and calling.

The yearlings that Krantz collected from the farms at that time of year derived without exception from cows other than ours. They were red, or had white socks and faces, or they might also be black-spotted and heavily horned: those were the most difficult to mate.

Once, I sat at the nursery window, it was my tenth year, watching the farmer and Krantz on the main road. They had clamped a hunk of birch around the yearling's neck so it wouldn't put up a fight; the dull sound of its front legs smacking and stumbling against the birch reached me all the way in the nursery. I sat behind Mam'selle Fanny's lace curtain, the sky was blue, no cloud in sight, a swirling infinity, and I eyed Krantz's tense neck and shoulders as he entered the courtyard, followed by the farmer and the yearling. Down by the pasture gate, Gustava looked pale. If the farmer misbehaved in the slightest in the courtyard, or if his eyes drifted for too long across Lilltuna's windows, the same farm wouldn't be used the following year. All was reported back to Doctor Eldh by Mam'selle Fanny, who stood on the hillside with the tobacco in her mouth and inspected the proceedings. That year, the farmer behaved himself and was not replaced. The yearling struggled with the clump that was meant to subdue him, right up until Krantz and the farmer unhooked it from him and withdrew as he was released into the pasture. Gustava stood, trampling, right outside the house, ashen under her grimy cap, and only when the yearling had been set loose and the gate to the pasture had been closed was she allowed to go back inside. I could hear her clomping around down there in her clogs, then running into the maid's room and sitting and snivelling for a long time with Hulda. After a while, they both came upstairs and unlocked the nursery door and sat with me during the mating because I had the best view: suddenly, both of them would be kind and obliging, and they'd bring boiled eggs with butter so as each to be granted a place beside me on my bed by the window. We watched the yearling out there among the cows. And Hulda drew me close and pressed me to her chest and sighed in dismay at the yearling's progress; I could feel the strawberry-red lumps squashed against my shoulders and smell the sour milk and fish broth on her hot breath, along with the fire of Gustava's glaring eyes under her cap. At first, the yearling merely stomped around the pasture, looking listless and confused, and then he grew stubborn. Krantz and the farmer walked around the wattle-fence ring on one side of the pasture and kept an eye on things in there. It was always the cow with the most tar on her rump with whom the bulls were the roughest. And yet the very next year, the day before the next yearling was to arrive, Krantz would still go around painting their rears in the stalls to make things gentler for

74

them. And each time, the bull went wild with the cows, and worked itself up, and squeezed the big tarred rumps between his forelegs, and slipped around on their knobbly backs, and the slim pink muscle underneath unsheathed itself like a long slippery knife of meat, and the cows roared in the pasture until late in the night. So it was this year, too. And Krantz had to drive the farmer back to his farm for the night so the bull would have time to do what he'd come to do. The farmers were never offered lodgings at Lilltuna. I sat in the fading afternoon with Hulda and Gustava and ate the eggs, my hands slick with butter, though as soon as Mam'selle Fanny returned to the house, they locked me back up and flung themselves down the stairs to the ground floor. At supper, Gustava again told the story of the boy rent in two, over where she had once been employed, how he was pinned to the barn wall by the bull and pushed around as his intestines spilled from his belly.

The pasture was quiet that night and the air was tense, as before a thunderstorm. I fell asleep with the pungent smell of tar in my nostrils, waking only after sunrise. By then the yearling had been caught and the birch clump refastened so he could be led home by Krantz and the farmer, and again, at Christmas, I was given a little piece of a calf-brown ear. The taste of buttered egg on the walls of my mouth. In the morning sun, the dew glinted on the grass between the cows as they rose after their long night in the pasture with the bull. In the winter of that year, Master Valdemar arrived.

We could have gone even further out, little Beda and I, that summer night. Survived on leaves and pine needles. Slept between the rocks, in pits we had dug for ourselves like the animals did under the spruces.

I was the Bandaged One: it was the long night of the Scrawny One. And then dawn rose above the pond, and Krantz appeared between the trees, and we were retrieved.

On the bench below the veranda, Hulda and Gustava were peeling potatoes as they watched us come into the courtyard, water dripping from Beda's hems as she slumped like a sack over the edge of the barrow that Krantz had put her in by the pond. As soon as we got to the house, it was as if my legs went soft, and I crumpled and fell. Then Krantz carried me in and up the stairs with Fanny behind, pressing bedclothes to her chest.

I was laid in bed, I was fed oat soup, I was stripped of my Sceptre and wadmal trousers; I closed my eyes as my face was washed clean of forest dirt, and the Bandage was peeled off me. I was dressed in plain-weave linen and pantalettes. September flies between the window panes, knees against the horse blanket. Beda picked up by a horse and carriage. White oval.

In the mornings after, as I lay in bed with my face to the wall, I could hear Gustava enter the nursery to empty the commode; once, she stood still for a long time behind me, breathing and lingering. *Caesaria,* she said, low and pleading, but I didn't reply and I did not turn around. I waited for the

Scrawny One, for her to come back to me from the night, I awaited further instruction:

And who hath the sceptre shall quench the fire of the dragon, and be delivered to the throne of heaven—

On the sixteenth day Doctor Eldh returned.

The ray between waking and sleeping. The snow arrived early and was abundant the winter Master Valdemar came to Lilltuna. Frozen crust on the snow. The walls crackling with cold. I lay in bed under three horse blankets; in the mornings, the tip of my nose was blue and aching. On the coldest nights Fanny came up and slept in my bed; we lay with our backs to each other to keep warm. I often rolled over in my sleep and she'd immediately roll me back and I'd wake up. It didn't matter: when I slept with Fanny, the cut-out creatures left me alone and sleep became dreamless and crystalline. Then, the night frost sang in the glass of the window. The metal in the toy trains and the windup ballerinas Doctor Eldh had given me turned cold as ice. He didn't come for Christmas like he'd said. When Krantz returned to Lilltuna with purchases from the city in the small sleigh strapped to the piebald, he brought a Christmas greeting, which he presented without removing his mittens, hastily written on a small card with stamped stars and Christmas roses:

Merry Christmas to you, Kitten!
Soon I will be home with my little girl again. Until then, enjoy Fanny's delightful Christmas ham out there at Lilltuna and remember to say your evening prayers.
Blessed greetings, Dr. E

When Fanny tired of coming up to give me warmth, I'd go and sleep beside her, down in the kitchen next to the wood stove. Her bed had been dragged there from the housekeeper's quarters, along with the maid's sofa for Hulda and Gustava, and the fire soon made the air stale and the kitchen sooty. In the evenings, Fanny told us to kneel at the edge of the bed and fold our hands in evening prayer. The cold rose from the tiles through the layers of rag rugs, up into our knees; it made our skin pucker and numbed our limbs. I recited Our Fathers and the assigned passages from the Psalter, and when my teeth chattered too loudly or I failed to sit still during prayer, Fanny reprimanded me with an open palm on my backside over my clothes, after which we went to bed. Hulda and Gustava lay head-to-toe on the sofa, and I on one side of Mam'selle Fanny's bed, and she read to us about the Lord Jesus and the lake of fire into which the Dragon Tempter was to be cast.

In the mornings, I dangled my legs over the edge of Fanny's bed while Gustava wrapped my shins and feet with strips of wool, then I put on ski boots that had been lined with straw so I could go skiing with Krantz between the poplars in the garden. He'd let me ski unleashed, and I could take the lead and create our path. A diamond-sharp light fell through the crystals of snow piled heavy on the branches of the garden trees. Krantz stank more than usual when skiing because he slept indoors with the animals in winter, in the barn where the lambs and chickens had been moved, where it became cozy and muggy, and a condensation settled on the dirty windows where I wrote my name, my fingertip slipping along the damp glass as he pulled on his ski boots. His hair was messy, even though he'd had Fanny cut it when she was performing one of her regular lice checks. If I came down to the barn too early and surprised him, he'd always get up from his bed in the same apologetic way and clumsily pull on his quilted trousers and look at me with fluttering eyes, the oblong stick jutting against the bottom of his shirt like a helpless finger, although he tried to hide it.

I'd immediately turn around and take a seat on the stump and wait and watch the white landscape until he came trudging through the snow, complete with his ski boots and fur hat. I'd ski through the narrowest gaps between the trees in the garden, and Krantz would find it difficult to follow, and I'd gain speed right up until he caught up with me. He'd always swerve and plant himself in front of me and block my path, the corner of his mouth twitching as he suppressed a triumphant smile.

He no longer poured out water for me to make the small ice rinks because I'd outgrown my skates, and I hadn't received new ones from Doctor Eldh, though I'd entered them on my wish list. It worried me that the doctor hadn't asked me to take the list out of the bedside drawer for a long time, nor had he replenished my toys and wardrobe. I sat at the desk in my room, practising my handwriting and speed writing, binding my chest tighter; when I unwrapped myself alone at night, the boils were lumpy and folded like lambs' ears. I waited for a reprieve, hoped that my skill with the pen would hasten the doctor's return. When the puss slunk into the kitchen to escape the cold, and Fanny poured fresh milk for her into a cracked dish, I would sit with her for a while as she drank. Then I'd stick my finger into the thick liquid as she lapped it up, and her rough tongue would run across it and I'd feel a strange throb and heat between my thighs.

At night, the cut-outs began to emerge again from the darkness and my sleep, even though I was downstairs with Fanny, though every so often I could tame and manipulate the dreams and escape the creatures as I dreamed them, and I would heave myself further into waking. But the taming provided only temporary relief, and other, more horrible images replaced the first. When it wasn't the cut-outs with their smooth, insistent faces, it could be the pond that appeared, first with an atmosphere of safety, the clear brown caress of water rippling and flowing across me, but then the pond would become a furious fire, blazing and sizzling my face and arms. At other times the pond became an unmoving eye, watching me unendingly, an indifferent body of water from which a ticking sound would suddenly arise, faint to begin with, then louder: the relentless seconds hammered away, and I could never be sure whether I'd succeed in waking and redirecting the image or if I'd tumble right down into that eye.

On Christmas Eve that year, Krantz drove Fanny and Hulda and Gustava in the big sleigh to Midnight Mass in the village. Fanny was wearing her fine fur coat, the black one. I stood in the nursery window and watched her disappear over the crest of the hill; she'd locked me in before leaving. A clear, starry night. A spruce tree, its lower branches stripped, adorning the front steps for yuletide. The baby Jesus was in the nativity crib, a gift from Doctor Eldh, though Fanny had removed the little gilded candles so I wouldn't catch fire in her absence, and the stove had been hasped and locked. I fiddled around with my toys in the nursery; I heard the fox scream at the forest edge; the embers in the stove waned and the room grew cold and raw. Over and again I read the doctor's Christmas greeting and the letter from the continent that I kept in the desk drawer. I fell asleep wrapped in the horse blanket on the floor next to the fireplace.

In the early hours of the morning, Krantz came in and carried me down to Fanny's bed in the kitchen, and I lay again with my back against that warm, bony body. When she got up and went to the privy, I heard Hulda whispering to Gustava on the maid's sofa that, while standing around on the church hill after mass, she'd heard that the doctor had indeed already come home, and, after that long trip abroad, was celebrating Christmas with gusto in the city with his daughters in the Eldh residence. And wasn't it a little strange, really, that he hadn't come out to Lilltuna yet? Though it was understandable, Hulda said, that Christmas should be celebrated with one's nearest, especially after such a long tour. I could hear the mocking chirp in Hulda's voice, as if she knew I was listening.

I fell asleep in the stuffy heat of the fire; I woke each time Fanny took me by the shoulders to turn me away from her.

New Year came, it was January.

I was still waiting for Doctor Eldh.

When I couldn't go back to sleep after Fanny had turned me, I'd often sit in the window with the horse blanket while the others were still sleeping. I'd see the fox scurry across the courtyard and the lynx roam outside the barn, where the tempting scent of chicken and lamb drifted through the plank wall. A black sky, strewn with stars. A half moon motionless over the snow-laden sheds and barns. Sometimes the wind blew hard through the courtyard, and on many nights the snow was wild and heavy, but there were times when it was perfectly still out there, clear white nights, the snow cover sparkling in the moonlight.

It was on one such wakeful night that I heard the call from out in the snow.

It came from the garden and sounded like the cries of fairy folk. I turned to the others, but no one moved, even though the wailing went on and on, and I was afraid it was coming from inside my own head. And then it paused, before a brief final cry was unleashed, and then everything went dead silent.

I waited a moment before putting on my ski boots and Fanny's coat in the entryway, taking a lantern and opening the kitchen door at the back of the house. I was walking in the knee-high snow, along the unshovelled path, when the barn door, which someone had closed sloppily, suddenly whipped shut in the wind; I jumped and stopped. Then I saw the trail, from the barn to the big elm at the top of the garden, and the big bundle up there that had been tossed onto the snow, and a dark swathe that spread across the ground. As I neared with the lantern, I saw that it was Krona the cow who'd collapsed there by the elm tree, and she had bled profusely until the seeping blood had formed a dark puddle all around her: she lay on her side, belly distended under her red coat, and the fuzzy head of the unborn calf was sticking out of her bottom. Its eyes were still closed, covered by Krona's membranes, its bluish tongue hanging askew from its muzzle; the calf had been strangled on its way out, if it hadn't already died inside, in the darkness of her body. I stood for a while with the lantern and looked at the calf and Krona: the light made the corner of the calf's eye glisten a bit, and as I walked around them, Krona's eyes glistened in the same way. As if tears could come from the dead, and the two of them were weeping.

I sat down on the mound next to it and the lantern flickered and went out, and it began to snow again: and after that, dawn came, and Krona was covered by the big powdery flakes as if this night of death had been vested in a heavenly garb. Then there was a slam from inside the barn and the door was thrown open. *Satan,* hissed Krantz, once he'd stomped drowsily over to me and Krona. The little unborn face with the closed eyelids was already hidden under the white blanket.

The snow poured down on Krantz all morning as he toiled under the elm and pushed Krona's body onto the wagon and rolled it back into the barn. I sat at the long table in the kitchen and ate the oat soup, I drank the lukewarm milk, I stood at the window and watched. The head sticking out of the back hung limp, gently swung and swayed, and the darkness twisted into Lilltuna until the trail in the snow that Krantz had made when moving Krona's body disappeared.

I LOVED IT WHEN sheet lightning struck at Lilltuna. I'd sit on the pile of wood inside the shed, my feet dangling, brown and summer-hard; I'd borrow Krantz's pocket knife and scrape my toenails clean. I could always sense when Doctor Eldh was coming to visit. I'd spit on a fold of my underskirt and rub my grimy face clean, looking into Krantz's shard of mirror in the barn; I'd put my summer shoes on. Sometimes the doctor took his time, but he would come in the end. I'd make a wreath of meadow flowers and place it over my loop braids; I'd avoid Krantz's dung piles so my clothes wouldn't smell; I'd lie on my stomach on the roof of the gazebo and stare at the main road. When the carriage arrived on the crest of the hill, I'd climb down and run to the front of the house, where Fanny would be standing on the steps, waiting for me, if she hadn't already hunted me down, my nice boots to hand. I waited patiently while the doctor got out and the carriage door shut with a bang. I curtsied, I accepted the pats on my head, I went up to the nursery and waited for him to summon me for my lessons. The smell of Fanny's coffee filled every room of the house, and, when I cracked open the nursery window, I heard the East India Company china clinking in the library below each time the doctor, seated on the ottoman, raised the cup to his lips. He liked to sit with the windows wide open: the first thing he did was to let the air billow into the room that had been shuttered in his absence. Not even Fanny was allowed to enter and dust the shelves and the glass ovals of his daughters' portraits when the doctor was away. He sat by the window with his coffee, he knew I was listening. After a while, he'd call to me, set the steel pen down on the walnut table with a soft click. I'd grab it immediately and dip its tip in the ink and put it to the paper, I'd look up at the doctor's face and wait for the words. The troubled summer sky beyond Lilltuna seethed. He always called me Kitten or Little Mongrel or My Heart; only after his crying would he say my real name. The flashes of lightning, the delays before the thunder rumbled through the garden. He'd leave the windows open, the casement latches in place, even as the rain poured into the room and rattled the windows, and I gave shape to letters with the steel pen on the paper while the water streamed down the frames and pooled on the floor, as if a flood were coming. I thought of the blessed light over Lilltuna, of the deer that flocked through the garden on balmy evenings, I thought of the scrawny one's pelvic bone, smoothened from touch and resting in Doctor Eldh's right-hand desk drawer. I pressed the pen between my index finger and thumb, I rasped letters in straight lines across the paper from the city, I wrote:

On the art of examination. For a bimanual examination during home visits, a simple table covered with a blanket can be used as an examination bed. The patient is laid on her back with her legs bent at the knees and hips and the feet placed on the lower end of the tabletop. The head and the upper part of the back are elevated with a pillow. Remove the stays, unbutton the waistband of the dress, and loosen all ties around the waistband so the clothing can be pulled down and the slip pulled up to expose the abdomen. After noting the abdomen's shape, a general physical examination with soundings-out of the body's surface is conducted: if there is a need for internal examination, forceps, speculum, tweezers, and curettes may also be used. It should be borne in mind that the question of a patient's most recent menses may at first occasion a misleading reply, owing to a guilty conscience or to fear of having been infected by recent coitus or defloration, thus complicating the examination. There are various but easily recognizable categories of patient, the archipelagos of which one can, with experience, surely navigate: the chatty; the modest; and the reluctant. Unmarried women in general proffer a greater deal of false information, although they know it will be discovered in the next moment of the examination. This holds true even in obvious cases, such as the insertion of foreign objects into the vagina—a not uncommon problem. If such is the case, and if an object has caused ulceration or fistulas, lancing devices and hot knives can be employed. Recovered objects have been various, and inserted with different intentions, such as for masturbatory purposes, for reasons of insanity, or with the aim of inducing criminal abortion: items have included hairpins, probes, catheters, iron pokers, pomade jars, bottles, parts of candlesticks, children's trumpets, spools of thread, pipe bowls, spoons, combs, scissor cases, toys, tufts from clothing or blankets, wooden sticks, cupboard knobs—

When the kitchen floor was at its sharpest cold, and Fanny was stirring the embers and clattering the dishes and kettles at the stove, Hulda rolled over on the maid's sofa, where she was lying head-to-toe with Gustava and whispered that I should be careful not to fall asleep with the myling nearby, the unwanted newborn scratching its bleeding nails from inside the secret grave its mother had made for it under the floor by my bed. Winter light. Strips of blue in the grainy white.

I folded my hands in evening prayer; I listened to Mam'selle Fanny read about the lake of fire. January went by.

It was in the evening, when Krantz had come in and stamped the snow from his boots, after the upheaval with Krona under the elm tree, that Gustava heard the covered sleigh coming down the road from the shed where she was looking for firewood. Whirling snow, the verge of a storm.

Fanny glanced first at Gustava, who stood flushed and breathless in the kitchen hallway, and then at Krantz, who kept his boots on and went out to the front with the lantern to have a look. I felt my heart pecking at my chest like a magpie chick, I ran my fingers along the edge of the bandage, I straightened my skirt over the scent of fish guts and death coming from the slit. As the sleigh slid into the unshovelled courtyard, I watched with Hulda and Gustava at the window. Our shadows removed themselves from the squares of light cast on the snowdrifts outside, and the coachman huddled on the box with his collars folded up while slowing the horses to a stop. Then its curtain was pushed aside, and Doctor Eldh climbed out. His cheeks were plumper after the long tour, and he wore earflaps under his top hat. The frost had pinched his eyebrows and whiskers; I couldn't make out his expression. He beckoned to Krantz, who put the lantern down on the kitchen steps, and they leaned into the coach and started rooting around inside, pulling at something in there.

Suddenly, the man who called himself Master Valdemar was stood in the courtyard in the snow, supported under his arms by Krantz and the doctor, his golden locks lolling. His eyes were hidden by his hair, no hat. As Krantz and the doctor laboured up to the house with the curly-locked man, he kept slipping and sliding in the powdery snow, his feet tucked into dainty evening boots with grubby gaiters on top. As they came closer, I could hear him sniggering and cackling, talking strangely and shrilly in Krantz's and then the doctor's ears; neither of them engaged with him but simply stared ahead with dogged countenances, slightly bent under his weight. When they were a few steps up the stairs, the tossing head suddenly lifted and the man's face was revealed. The face smiled, big and drowsy, and stared right at me through the window, with its glassy green eyes fringed with pale lashes. I couldn't tell if he was looking at me or through me: for a moment I was slung into the infinity of those dark kernels. When Fanny opened the door, snow cascaded into the entry-way, and she dashed to the cupboard to fetch piles of linens and blankets while Krantz and the doctor and the curly-locked man came into the kitchen corridor. And, while hurrying by, she ordered Hulda and Gustava to carry a bed into the library and light the fire in the stove.

While it was still warming up in there, the curly-locked man lay in the kitchen, on Fanny's bed, which he had dropped onto with Krantz's help. He was lying on his back, his arms flung out across the edges of the bed, his mouth open, already asleep. I sat on the bench next to Krantz and Doctor Eldh, and we ate Fanny's veal soup. The doctor's fingers were red and chapped with cold. The clouds of whiskers, the inscrutable profile. He slurped up the last of the soup. He hadn't given me my pat on the head. Done with his meal, he went over to Fanny and they exchanged a few inaudible words, their heads turned away, and I bent deeper over my soup; then the doctor went to lay down in his chamber, which had also been heated for the night.

He who called himself Master Valdemar stayed in the kitchen with his soiled gaiters and his arms extending from his body like a crucifix. I observed the lines of his beardless chin and the frost-blooms on his cheeks; sleep made the closed eyelids of his finely cut face twitch arrhythmically. Then, on his own, Krantz rose from his emptied bowl of soup and lugged that lifeless body away from Fanny's bed. He dragged the curly-locked man into the library, where he dropped him on Fanny's clean linens and pulled off his drenched gaiters and evening boots. I stood in the doorway and studied the man's pale feet, with their swirls of curly hair, quivering and glittering reddish-gold in the light from the sconces. His toes looked long and funny, almost like fingers. The nails were clipped. The curly-locked man grunted a little in his sleep, like a horse or a small child. When I lay down with my back to Fanny in the bed in the warmth of the kitchen, the curly-locked man had left a whiff of snaps and rosewater in the blanket. The sound of the mice scrabbling and scampering in the cupboards. That was the first night.

THE DREAMS I HAD up in my nursery as a child were never the same but similar. There was the recurring fiery eye from which the sound of a ticking clock could become deafening; the black-haired sisters who waved at me from across the water; the skinny monsters that wrapped their claws and fingers around me and against whom I was defenceless, since I was the one who'd brought them out of the darkness, as one cuts dolls from a sheet of paper or a cloth.

And there were other dreams: quieter, equally recurring. In one, I was walking through the house, which had been inexplicably emptied of furniture, and in the middle of the drawing-room I noticed a strange plant protruding from the floorboards: the plant was rose-like and black with large velvety leaves, and the moment I bent down to pick from it, it fell apart and smeared across my fingers like wet ash. In another, I was standing in the potato field and saw a human shape far off on the horizon, but as I approached, it seemed to disappear, and where the field ended was simply white, a thick and grainy void. I drove my hand into the whiteness, then I woke up. In a third, I was standing with a dissecting knife in my hand, cutting through a body of indeterminate shape, its skin stretched thin over bones and intestines, the gnarled contours of which could be discerned underneath; when the incision was large enough, I plunged my hand straight into the cut and retrieved nothing but sheer cold from the interior cavity: in the moment I removed my hand from the hole, it was covered in frost and ice, and when I bent a finger, my hand shattered like the most fragile of glass.

After his arrival with the curly-locked man at Lilltuna, Doctor Eldh stayed only one night before going back to his work and to his daughters in the city. Heat hazed over the estate on the morning after his arrival; it wasn't snowing anymore. The doctor sat in the drawing-room, where he had been served jasmine tea and Gustava's wheat buns with a dab of butter and quince compote, then he called for Mam'selle Fanny and asked her to close the door behind her. I stood in the hallway outside, my feet double-socked; I sat for a while on the floor with the *Flora* and my notebook. I could hear the doctor's and Fanny's voices talking with shapeless words. Master Valdemar was still asleep, under the East Indian wall clock, wrapped in Fanny's furs. When I got tired of eavesdropping, I went outside. I made three snowmen with the packed snow that had accumulated in the night, after the cold had eased, then I kicked them to pieces, one by one, the great tits gathering for the bread crumbs I'd used for their eyes and mouths. Inside, under the drawing-room chandelier, I saw Fanny appear, sat across from the doctor, her face turned away from the window; I could only see the back of the doctor's silver mane through the fogged-up panes between the grilles. I went to the barn. Krantz was sitting on the bench with his ski boots laced up; he looked troubled or pitying. He handed me the pair of skis the doctor had given me last Christmas, then I cut a trail through the snow, which hardened quickly and became slick and smooth, and we skied back and forth through the garden all morning. From a distance I saw the green lamp burning in the darkness of the library, and below the veranda, on the bench, the coachman leaned against the wall in a cloud of pipe smoke while he waited for the doctor, raising his pipe in greeting when Krantz and I skied back toward the house. The sun withdrew into the clouds while in the gloaming the snow gave off a matte, grainy sheen. Then I stood on the front steps and received my farewell pat on the head. Doctor

Eldh's hands were gloved and the gesture was distracted. He hadn't asked me to sit with him or play the square piano for him; he hadn't told me to come in and eat with him in the drawing-room. He smiled kindly and distantly at me as he settled into his sleigh. *Goodbye then, Kitten,* he said, and *until soon.* Then he drew the curtain across the opening of the hood, and the sleigh took the curve across the courtyard and disappeared. The rim of light at the edge of the sky before the afternoon darkness swept through Lilltuna. In the evening, I poked around in my egg soup at the long table in the kitchen, while Fanny placed the plate of calf's feet on a tray and poured a splash of sloeberry wine into a crystal glass before carefully taking the curly-locked man's dinner into the library. I fell asleep to the sound of Hulda and Gustava's half-muffled chatter on the maid's sofa, not thinking about the new skates the doctor had forgotten.

The curly-locked man managed to sleep for a week out at Lilltuna before Hulda and Krantz took the little sleigh to town to do the purchasing. He brought no attention to himself, the library was silent, but from outside I could see through the windows that the lamp burned throughout the day. The dawn light was billowing and grey, as Krantz loaded the sleigh by the kitchen steps with the empty baskets and sacks. Hard snow. Hulda stared at me from the coach box; her face was white and round like a mocking moon, sticking out of the bulky winter shawl she'd wrapped around her head several times.

Later that day I practised the piano with my gloves on. It jangled and squealed horribly; it had been a long time since the doctor had brought the piano tuner out to Lilltuna. At mealtimes, Fanny went into the library with the trays of filled plates; she always pushed the door shut firmly behind her, and the trays were empty each time she re-emerged.

When Krantz and Hulda returned on the sleigh in the late afternoon, I stood on the kitchen steps again and watched Krantz, who unloaded the full baskets while Hulda lingered under her blanket, a sack of flour in front of her, her face as if she were sucking on an invisible caramel. She looked at me with a secretive expression before Krantz hissed at her to hurry up and get out and help: that's when I knew she had something important to tell me from the city.

And later, in the kitchen, in the evening, after Fanny had disappeared down the corridor with supper for the curly-locked man, and Hulda was sat on the bench next to Gustava, plucking the feathers out of a chuck, she burst out that, my, hadn't she heard a thing or two about the curly-locked man in town. She interrupted her plucking for a moment, her eyelids lowering and a contemptuous smile smearing across her face, and she slowed each tug teasingly before going on. I was rocking on my coccyx, sat on top of the pile of wood next to the door with my boots on; outside was pitch black, and the logs crackled and burned in the fireplace.

And what did Hulda hear in town? Gustava asked into the silence, her eyes slightly wider, and after a while she added: Oh, wouldn't kind Hulda be gracious enough to immediately impart what she had heard at once before Gustava loses her head? Then Hulda pensively licked the corner of her mouth with the pink tip of her tongue, like a scrappy cat, before saying that the curly-locked man was, apparently, a distinguished and very important gentleman from Copenhagen. Who had come as a guest and stranger to the city last autumn. And that this gentleman, who went by the name Master Valdemar, was truly of the rare and unusual kind. For, from what Hulda could glean from the people she knew and dealt with at the market stalls, the guest had, almost upon arrival at the start of autumn, become something of a celebrity there in the city. He had made himself infamous to all and sundry, among both the gentry and the common people; yes—she cast a long glance at me from across the kitchen—the master had made quite a few friends and acquaintances, among them Doctor Eldh. Who apparently, it had now been made clear to Hulda, had already returned from his long tour of the continent to the city in early September. And nonetheless he had waited until now to come to Lilltuna. He had stayed with his daughters in town all autumn, with this Master Valdemar as his new-found friend.

I glanced at Hulda, my heels thudding against the chunks of wood. She rested her hands on the chuck's breast for a moment before adding that this master, who now lay sleeping in the doctor's library, was also rumoured to be a friend and favourite of the Copenhagen court, where he'd held the post of Master of the Court Orchestra, or was he the court painter? Here the rumours diverged somewhat. Gustava moved closer.

And someone had told her, Hulda said, as she had walked between the market stalls by Krantz's side, that no one quite knew whether the curly-locked man was visiting the city to seek rest after his successes at court, or whether, as someone claimed, he had found himself at odds in Copenhagen and was now in exile, or whether, as others said, he was in fact no friend of the court, but a count, and a Frenchman, and on top of everything else unmarried, but most of this was loose talk and unsubstantiated. Hulda had that feline glint. And then what? Gustava urged. Well, Hulda said, whatever the case, in the late autumn this curly-locked man, who called himself Master Valdemar, through the acquaintances he'd made in the city, had been asked to lead one of the finer orchestral arrangements— Here Hulda swallowed, and was about to continue, when suddenly a door in the hallway slammed and Fanny appeared in the kitchen.

The wood dug into my buttocks. Outside, the stars were

bright, and under my skin was a sting and a glow that came with the thought of the curly-locked man and Doctor Eldh; waves of unease burned and shot through my limbs. Hulda held her tongue while Fanny went about her duties in the kitchen before bedtime. I drank the evening milk; I put on my nightclothes and tucked my loop braids under my cap. I lay under the covers in Fanny's bed with Hulda's contemptuous eyes on my nape, and whenever I looked over my shoulder, she looked away, her grin pasted between her ears.

Only once Hulda had nestled under the blankets, next to Gustava on the maid's sofa, and Fanny was visiting the privy, did she continue her story. Her voice sounded hoarse and urgent while she said, in a half whisper, that, all in all, this curly-locked man had indeed seemed particular and unusual in every way. So, when he had been invited to lead the orchestra at Baroness Gyllenclou's music salon, where the gentlemen of the Society of Sciences went to mingle and drink punch after their meetings, no one had raised an eyebrow, and all had taken it for granted: the curly-locked man had himself told them that he was a prominent kapellmeister from Copenhagen, with many recommendations and merits.

And then the following had occurred: on the evening in question, while the gentry and Society members had flocked into the splendid apartment of the baroness, and the orchestra were tuning their instruments, the curly-locked man had walked around with her and received the guests. Then he had walked up and down the aisle between the chairs placed in the hall, his gloved hands clasped behind his back, all the while nodding to one or another of the arrivals, almost as if the occasion were his own. The baroness had at first glanced around at this unexpected behaviour but then composed herself and allowed the curly-locked man to walk on in the hall and, as it were, oversee how everything was taking shape, and who was present, and whether they were sitting comfortably on the chairs, and if the hall was yet full. When this was done, the curly-locked man had, at last, resolutely walked up the aisle and taken his place before the orchestra, his back to the audience. There he had stood, motionless and without turning around, with both arms lowered and his eyes closed, no baton in his hand. And the small talk had faded away behind the curly-locked man, who looked more and more like a statue, and he had stood as still as this until the buzzing and the hawking stopped entirely, and the auditorium was silent but for the rustling of tails and bustles. All this had been detailed to Hulda by an acquaintance, a maid who had been on duty that evening and at that moment had been balancing a tray of refreshments by a wall. And the maid had said that a peculiar mood had descended upon the hall as a result of the curly-locked man's surprising behaviour—that he had simply stood in that way, with his eyes shut, for such a long time, dragging the moment out until it seemed endless.

The faces of the members of the orchestra had at first appeared tense and expectant as they gazed at the curly-locked man, ready with their instruments: apparently, he'd refused to rehearse the piece earlier in the day on grounds of artistic integrity, and had appeared at the baroness's home only shortly before the evening was to begin. But when, after the unusually prolonged moment, and despite the silence, the curly-locked man had yet to move or make the slightest suggestion of commencing, members of the orchestra began to look around, and one gave a laugh but fell silent again, and for a long time this was all that happened: the curly-locked man just stood there, between audience and orchestra. And there was the rasping of instruments and a tinkling, and a bow accidentally nudged the strings of a violoncello, whereupon the cellist first looked terrified and then stared in embarassment at his boots.

And the silence of the place had become dense and uneasy. There was a rustling here and there in the hall, and cold shivers ran down Hulda's acquaintance's spine because of the shocking nature of the situation, and her arms ached something terrible from holding the tray. Then, at last, as if from an invisible cue, the curly-locked man slowly began to raise his hands in the air, and, opening his fingers like two crowns or hoes, he let them rise above the top of his head, almost as if he were holding up a small suckling, Hulda's acquaintance had said, as if he were lifting a child toward the light of the crystal chandelier, toward a sun. The silence was now truly unbearable, for no one—neither in the orchestra nor the audience—had ever before witnessed this particular mode of conducting, if that was in fact what the curly-locked man was doing. And didn't he seem a little strange in the head, the staff had gossiped among themselves afterwards in the kitchen, and wasn't it a bit daft, this matter of the curly-locked man's hands, raised as they were in such devotion to the heavens, as if he were holding a treasure: yes, wasn't there something a bit overblown and almost make-believe going on in the baroness's salon, the kitchen wondered, but no one could quite put a finger on it. For a while, as the curly-locked man had stood there making a show of himself, the gentry had sat on their chairs as if bewitched, and some had opened their mouths wide, and fanned themselves with their plumes, all the while following the master's movements, as gentlefolk do when they've been patiently waiting for something surprising and rare. Then, the man sitting at the piano, looking frightened, his eyes fixed on the curly-locked man, had suddenly struck the first note. And the rest of the orchestra had tentatively but promptly joined in. And then the curly-locked man, his eyes still shut, had begun to draw and wave his hands in the air in a manner never before seen, and the question of whether this represented great

98

artistry or something quite different suddenly became pale and immaterial. For the piece went on to be played with a force that made the walls of the Gyllenclou salon quake. And Hulda's acquaintance's arms ached horribly, and, afterwards, when the curly-locked man finally turned to the audience and bowed in every direction and many times, the applause seemed never to want to end: Hulda's friend had not been able to sleep a wink for all the mental agitation and the shoulder ache. And behind the master sat the orchestra, their hairlines glistening with sweat, confusion drawn across their faces. The softly chiselled features of the curly-locked man seemed to shimmer in the light of the chandelier, and those green eyes gleamed below his swirling forelocks.

At the subsequent supper, when Hulda's acquaintance was rushing between the tables with the others, waiting on the guests, she saw the curly-locked man engaged in lively and intimate conversation, and an extraordinary atmosphere surrounded him.

Well into the winter, the master continued to lead the orchestra at the Baroness Gyllenclou's salon. And each time the music became more beguiling. And still he refused to participate in any rehearsals. During the day he could be seen walking through the city in his shiny topper, in the company of one of the members of the Society or some other gentleman, absorbed in conversation under a cloudy sky; November was now slipping into December. The snow arrived.

And at Christmas, Hulda's acquaintance was called in as an extra maid for the celebrations in the Eldhs' residence, where she once more had the chance to see the curly-locked man up close.

There were many guests, no expense had been spared, and, after the Christmas supper, during the cognac, as she dashed with trays and dishes through the rooms, she glimpsed him in the midst of a big crowd, flanked by Doctor Eldh's two daughters as he recounted his experiences at the court, or some other peculiar thing he said he had experienced during his travels down on the continent. The man who called himself Master Valdemar was a charmer; Hulda's acquaintance could see this much. He was always surrounded by female company. Which seemed to appeal to Doctor Eldh, who sat in the large leather armchair in the corner with his punch cup, listening from across the room to the curly-locked man, who in turn would meet the doctor's gaze with his green eyes and an amiable smile. The curly-locked man was instantly captivating, Hulda's acquaintance had said: it was simply such. On one occasion, she had passed him on her way to the kitchen as he smoked with Doctor Eldh by an open window. The two had looked amused and open-hearted. As she'd passed by, the acquaintance had heard the doctor say something to the effect that a scientist and composer are similar in many respects, for they both have to submit to their search for the unknown. That the difference between the human body and the manufactured musical organ was not as great as one might first imagine: they both required the right touch and great acuity of mind from their deliverer, so their messages could be captured and imparted to the world in the form of new and untold knowledge. The curly-locked man had taken a few quick puffs on his cigar and nodded behind the smoke.

After that, and several times during the Christmas festivities, the curly-locked man had often been seen coming to sit with the doctor's daughters by the fire and revel and tell tales; he'd become almost like a son, there in the Eldh residence, it was said.

Hulda fell silent.

I swallowed.

The wind frisked across the yard and set one of the barn hatches flapping; Fanny had still not returned from the privy.

And Hulda was no longer whispering when she added that, shortly after the new year came in, something suddenly changed with the curly-locked man. Or so her friend claimed. One evening, he hadn't shown up as expected to his appointment at the Gyllenclous'. And nor did he ever appear there again. Messenger boys were dispatched to the apartment where he lived but reported upon their return that the place was dark and no one had come to the door. And then other rumours began to swirl in the kitchens and in the marketplace, such as that the curly-locked man—having secured his name that autumn and winter in the city, and following his musical successes, and his diligent socializing with the most important figures among the gentry—well, he had also begun to rove the streets, in the autumn evenings as they slid into winter: alone. He'd begun to sit late into the night in alehouses and inns, warming himself in the cheaper taverns, and soon every farmhand and day labourer in town knew who the curly-locked man was. And there was chatter that the curly-locked man kept dubious nighttime companions, and girls, in the apartment in which he'd been invited to install himself at the expense of his patrons—for he had acquired these in his dealings in the city—one of whom was Doctor Eldh, and on one occasion a caretaker with whom Hulda was acquainted had passed below the windows of that apartment and had heard strange goings-on from inside the curly-locked man's abode, things one would rather not discuss or repeat. The caretaker had stopped and looked up at the building, for such sounds suggested that it might fall to him to come to somebody's aid, and with that thought he had seen a gloved hand reach out of the window and pull it shut, muffling the sounds but making them no less alarming: a great howl then came from inside, mournful, or pleading, and half-suffocated, or as if the curly-locked man were keeping animals in his rooms.

But what was there to say about this, other than the usual things that were said and that passed from the kitchens to the market stalls. And then came that particular evening, a short while into the new year, when the curly-locked man had not appeared, and then had ceased to materialize at the baroness's evenings altogether, while the curtains in the master's apartment remained drawn, morning and night.

From this point onward, neither Hulda's acquaintance nor the caretaker heard anything more.

But, Hulda said, over on the maid's sofa, her voice shrill and triumphant, never mind that, because she herself had since managed to uncover and piece together the true course of events, hadn't she now? For only the other day, the night before, in fact, when the doctor had arrived with the master at Lilltuna, she'd wrapped a pretzel from the kitchen in her skirt and gone out to sit for a while with the doctor's hired coachman, who was on the bench with his pipe, awaiting the doctor's command to drive him back to the city. And she had given the coachman the pretzel, a gift, and as such she had had the chance to talk to him, and she'd been able to put a thing or two together.

It sounded like she was smiling over there in the dark. Before she went on, she said that this coachman had been hired by the doctor on the evening they'd arrived on short notice, having been promised a not inconsiderable sum: in the first instance, simply to hitch the horse to the covered sleigh and drive the doctor from the Eldh residence to the curly-locked man's lodging, which he had. The January snow in the city had been powdery, and the snowfall had been increasing, as if a storm were building, and the coachman had waited for the doctor in the sleigh down on the street, outside the curly-locked man's apartment. The doctor had disappeared through the entrance of the building but emerged only a few minutes later, beckoning, from across the street, the coachman, who had tossed a few coins to a couple of passing children in return for guarding the sleigh, and then he'd trotted behind Doctor Eldh up the narrow stairs to the curly-locked man's floor. Inside, it was dark and gloomy, and, at first, the coachman had seen nothing, but once his eyes grew accustomed to the darkness, he noted that the apartment was in great disarray, and in the middle of the floor of the main room lay the curly-locked man. He looked filthy but was in evening dress from head to toe, chuckling and cackling to himself. The doctor had not said a word to the coachman, other than that he should hold the master under the armpits and pull him to his feet. After which the doctor himself had taken hold of the master, too, and the two men had helped him down to the street. There, they thrust him into the sleigh as best they could and covered him with a pelt to shield him from the cold. The coachman could see that the curly-locked man's face was bluish and dark, from the snaps or from some other unknown shadow.

Then the sleigh had slipped through the alleyways, among the swirls of white flakes that now filled the air, and left the city behind. And on the country roads the darkness had been thick and compact, and the sleigh's lanterns had bobbed and swayed with the vehicle's every toss and turn, slinging fitful swathes of yellow light across the snow.

I SLEEP WITH MY body pressed to the stove; I have sealed the windows against the cold. Some days, the winter sun finds its way to the floor tiles through the gaps in the curtains, making the dust motes glow as they drift to the floor in those slim pillars of light.

Night birds.

Sometimes, when Doctor Eldh visited, I would sit beside him and look out at the trees and pasture through the open library window. I was five years old, I was six and seven, nine. The hogweed trembled in the wind out in the English garden. Yellow daylight or pale turquoise.

During those times by the window, the doctor often looked melancholy or pensive. My rump would chafe through my skirt against the hard stool, but I did not move. If the light from outside was bright enough in that dark room, I might turn and regard the glass of the East Indian wall clock. The reflection from the square of the clock's window looked like a painting in miniature, slightly domed by the glass, framed by the whorls and shells and small sharp leaves and rosettes of the gilded case: a painting of Lilltuna. The damp in the clock's wood caused the gold to flake along its curves, but the doctor never brought a craftsman or watchmaker from the city to tend to it; he let it flake. I'd sneak glimpses at his face as we sat, staring out of the window at the pasture and a sliver of the hillside fields, forever trying to imagine which gestures and questions the doctor preferred, how near or far he wished me to be.

Why do the leaves of the birch tree fall in winter but not the needles of the spruce, Doctor Eldh? I asked.

Because of the passage of time and the disparate nature of the two, he answered evasively.

When does the small child stop being a child? I then asked.

Once infinity has escaped her, the doctor replied.

On the occasions when he took me by the hand, and summoned his accompanying coachman, and asked him to drive us out into Lilltuna's surrounding countryside, the doctor always folded up the top so I wouldn't be glimpsed. He opened the old *Flora* in my lap, then I was to match the illustrations in the book with the plants we saw in the ditches we drove past. On a few occasions he'd ask the driver to stop at a meadow and we would sit in the tall grass. Then I might pluck small bouquets of wildflowers, which later, in the library, after we returned from our excursion, I'd place between the pages of Doctor Eldh's medical encyclopedia, going on to paste the flattened plant parts in the notebooks he brought me from the city. There in the meadows, the doctor would lean against a rock, over which he'd draped his coat, and fall asleep as I went about my picking; from a distance I could study that huge face as he slept. Doctor Eldh's sleep was often troubled with sudden, intangible movements that drew across his large, domed features and caused his eyeballs to cast about behind those thin eyelids. Down in the valley lay Lilltuna: the roof tiles of the main house flashing in the sun, the barn and the sheds and Krantz's dung heaps, the dairy animals slumped heavily on the grass in the pasture.

I could have stood up and called to the coachman, sitting on the box a little way off, dozing with a blade of grass in his mouth. I could have told him about Lilltuna, and the library with the East Indian wall clock, and about my Creation. Then he might have looked up at me, there on the box, eyes wide with horror, and held out his hand and told me to get in, and driven me away in the carriage while the doctor lay asleep. But I sat beside Doctor Eldh and tied up little wild-flower bouquets while he slept; I adjusted my bonnet so the sun wouldn't blind me; I didn't go over to the coachman. I waited for the doctor to open his eyes: I always had the sense that time stood still when he was sleeping. When finally he awakened, there in the meadow, he'd look at me with a drowsy, crooked, and somehow penitent smile, and he'd half whisper my name with a smattering of surprise, as if it were dawning on him, like a riddle from a dream he'd just solved. *Surely you'll forgive me,* he might say again in that muddled voice: *Surely you'll forgive me after all?*

I'd squint uncomprehendingly at him in the glittering sun. I'd smile and hand him the bouquet.

Then the doctor would look relieved and reinvigorated and give my braid a little tug, and he'd get up from the meadow, his trousers wrinkled and stained at the seat by the grass and earth, and we'd take the carriage back down to the house. In the evenings, after he'd gone back to his daughters in the city, I'd fall asleep in the nursery with my head full of bluebells and daisies, marguerites, clover flowers, cornflowers, lady's mantle, cow parsnip, bindweed, rattle, wood avens, early marsh orchid, spiked speedwell, forget-me-nots, purple gentian, carnations, windflower, wintergreen, honeysuckle, fluffweed, comfrey, rock cinquefoil, milkwort, thistle, mint, teasel, and violets—

The cold eased. The doctor was still to return following the evening he had brought Master Valdemar to Lilltuna in the sleigh. The stove pattered when its embers burst. Outside, the furrowed earth lay monotonously, like bars of a grate. Chalk-white shreds of cloud moved across a bright yellow sky. I went sledding in the last of the snow on Krantz's wood-plank skis, the icicles now falling from the roofs and dripping into the rain barrels; I was sent back to sleep in my own bed upstairs. There were times when I heard stirrings from the library as I tended to my errands, passing its closed door: the thud of a dropped object; footsteps across the rug. Every so often, I encountered Fanny with a tray as I stood in the hallway; she always gave me a look that made me turn right back around. The hard winter grass was matted and grey after the weight of the snow, the poplars in the garden were bald and black. I collected kindling and put it in the shed to dry; I built a labyrinth of twigs on the hill; I no longer sat with my notebook at the desk and practised my handwriting. Holes appeared in the dresses that Doctor Eldh had bought for me on his travels; they strained across my back as I sat at the piano in the evenings at Fanny's request. I played songs and waltzes, I wore my gloves: the cold in the house was still raw, the keys icy, but they warmed the more deftly I played. The square piano whined; the doctor didn't come, nor did the piano tuner. The days passed. Fanny hurried up and down the corridor with the trays for Master Valdemar, loaded with leg of lamb and potato stew, ham and liver soup, afterwards, the coffee cup with a splash of punch. At supper, Hulda watched me from across the kitchen table, a birdlike smirk tugging at the corner of her mouth. I squelched through the wet snow in the garden; I let my wool skirt soak up to my knees. Sunlight flooded the courtyard and my room.

March now.

One afternoon, as I was walking back to the house from the garden, Master Valdemar was sitting on the slope below the veranda. He was on one of the garden chairs, his body wrapped in Mam'selle Fanny's blankets, and his hands clasped a cup of steaming tea. I had not laid eyes on him since the evening of his winter arrival. His fingers were as long as prehensile claws, just like his toes. Otherwise he looked haggard and pale, and his green gaze tracked me as I approached the house. *You play beautifully,* he said when I was close enough, his voice bright and unusual, his words laboured, with the hint of an accent. I stopped and curtsied briefly in the master's direction before going to my oat soup. That evening, when I sat to play at the square piano, I suddenly heard the wall clock ticking from inside the library, where the door was now ajar, and I knew that time had again been set in motion. He who called himself Master Valdemar was walking around in there; it sounded as if he were rummaging through the doctor's bundles of papers and manuscripts on the otherwise bare shelves, and there was the gentle clink of porcelain. I tried to imagine his face, his back straightening in his chair, the curls of hair at his hairline; perhaps he sat down for a moment on the stool where I was usually told to sit during my lessons. I thought of how I'd sat at the walnut table with the goose quill and the scented papers, opposite Doctor Eldh; I thought of the domed eye of the clock turned in toward its own eternity. I placed my fingers on the piano keys. I removed my gloves, even though the March chill still gnawed at the walls, and with that I played.

WHEN I WAS STILL a small child, I was given a lamb. That was when I'd still sit in Fanny's embrace in the evenings, on the glass-roofed veranda, drinking warm milk, when she hadn't yet begun to send me back to bed, and to sit over on the rocking chair, drowning out the sound of me with her readings about the Lord Jesus Christ; when I was still allowed to fall asleep enveloped in a haze of tobacco and lavender and Fanny's skin. I still milled around then, close to her, while she tended to her chores, clinging to her skirt and asking to sit in her lap: and Fanny would pick me up and hold me. I sat at her feet with the cloth rabbit and the doll with the silk crinoline while she lost herself in her embroidery, and every time I wanted to be with her, she put aside whatever she was doing. Then I was given the lamb. It was Krantz who came to the house one evening, with the little black creature draped over his arm, to ask Fanny what to do with it; the lamb was small and strangely thin and had been rejected, first by the ewe who'd birthed it, and then by the other ewes who'd been there with the milk lambs down in the pen. Fanny lifted the lamb, which hung slack in the crook of Krantz's arm and bleated softly, and she declared that she and I would become the lamb's new mothers. Its coat was dark and glossy, almost blue, and it swirled across its bony body in smoothly composed patterns. Fanny pointed to the lamb and said to me: *You see, girl, how the Lord God creates all the beautiful and intricate things here in this world?* As I sat on the glass veranda with the lamb, feeding it the milk Fanny had poured into a small glass jar with a handmade spout, the sun sank over the bowed roof of the woodshed and the twilight fell, yellow and warm and strange upon us. The lamb only wanted to drink for brief spells and often turned its curly, sluggish head away, every now and then staring from my lap into the trees in the garden as if it were waiting for something. I would set it down on the floor, and the lamb would take a few steps across Fanny's rag rugs, but then it would sit back on its haunches and bleat, wanting only to stay put. For four nights I slept in the kitchen with Fanny while the lamb rested on the linens she had piled up for it on the floor beside me. Fanny slept deeply, whereas I woke up with the lamb's every bleat and movement, and I'd reach my hand over the edge of the bed and cup its crooked withers, patting there until it quieted. On the fifth day, I woke up and the bed made of linens was empty and the lamb had been removed. And Fanny gave me oat soup, and dressed me in my pinafore, and tightened the braids at my nape, and all the while I asked her where the lamb had gone. At last, her face pinched, she said that not every beautiful thing in this world was allowed the gift of life: *'Tis a pity, child,* but I wasn't to ask about it again. Her explanation did not satisfy me: I stayed at Fanny's heels all day, asking about the lamb until she tired of me and put me in the corner, but then I lay on the rag rugs for a long time, creasing my dress and screaming for the lamb. Fanny and her pinched face stayed bent over her chores and she held her tongue, until at last she let go of everything in her hands except the wooden spoon and took three strides across the floor and reprimanded me. In the evening, I lay in my bed in the nursery and sobbed for the lamb and for Fanny, and she locked me inside and went down the stairs to Krantz and supper. I heard the woodpecker out on a pine, I screamed myself hoarse, I fell asleep with my pinafore on, and in the morning the bed was wet and sticky when Fanny came up. She sat for a while on the edge of the bed, her back to me, and the morning sun played at her nape across the loose bun where wisps of her salt-and-pepper hair had come loose. Then she turned around and stroked my forehead and cheeks and said: *Poor silly thing, what life is this for a child?* And she lifted me out of the bed and pulled the sticky clothes off me and stripped the bed and carried me down the stairs to the kitchen, where she put me in the bathing tub. She left the oat soup on a low flame and undid my braids and poured hot water over me, the ladle resting on the crown of my head. Outside, the woodpecker kept drilling into the pine trees and the trill echoed and mingled strangely with the rippling water as the afternoon sun moved slowly across the floor. Coral-red light. I was cleaned, I was dried, I ate: I stopped asking about the lamb.

Sometime later, once Fanny had begun to leave me upstairs in the nursery again and would send me away from her bed, the lamb began to call me from the courtyard at night. At first I simply covered my ears with the pillow, but the lamb bleated loudly and shrilly outside and couldn't be silenced. Finally I went down in my stockinged feet and nightdress and looked for the lamb that was calling for me so desperately but didn't want to reveal itself in the summer night, and then I went into the pen. There, the sheep crowded together with their half-grown litter of lambs, who were already looking clumsy and ugly, and they stared at me, and I felt as if they were hiding the little lamb from me, behind their backs, just to torment me. And I went in among them to retrieve the lamb, whose bleating was shrill and jarring to my ears, but behind them the space was empty: gaping. Then the fox barked from the edge of the forest, as if the both of us had been reached by the lamb's cry. I started elbowing and pushing the sheep and as-yet lambs, forcing them further out into the courtyard, brandishing an old manure shovel while they trotted into the night. Some stalled, sticking to the garden's edges, and wouldn't let themselves be urged onward, but I got several of them to trot further, into the forest. When I ran out of energy, I returned to the house and up the stairs to my room and lay down on the bed and listened to the barking fox, which had finally silenced the lambs. And, toward dawn, the door of the farmhand's cottage banged downstairs, and Krantz darted across the gravel. I sat in the kitchen and ate Fanny's morning gruel while I listened to Krantz cursing outside, crossing the courtyard with the remains of the sheep's riven bodies and returning the rest to the pen. Fanny had her back to me at the stove; she stirred the kettle and said nothing. I brought the ladle of gruel to my lips; inside my head, the silence sang. The scent of fur and burnt meat rose from Krantz's fire out in the meadow, under the churning sky, and evening came.

My FIRST IMAGES OF Lilltuna: hazy sunlight filtering through a window, the scent of clean linen. I had brown hair, I had soft palms, I toddled down the front steps to Doctor Eldh as soon as he opened the carriage door. Then he lifted me high into the air and spun me around, before going into the library and opening the windows wide and then standing in front of the wall clock, gently prodding its interior to set time back in motion. The doctor's broad back obscured the clock face, but I could hear springing and snapping inside its golden case as he pushed the hands around, then shut the door, never touching the rounded glass.

While he worked, the doctor always let me play on the carpet with the little horse he'd given me for Christmas. I lay on my stomach with the atlas and practised the names of the countries; I sat across from him at meals in the drawing-room and put my fork to my mouth and ate the fish pudding. Outside, rose-coloured twilight split the evening in two. Crows or magpies cawing in the lindens around the back. I sat in my sailor costume with my arithmetic book open and the wall clock above me; it was a comfort and a fright that its unseeing eye continued to watch over me.

Doctor Eldh stood at the library window contemplating the sky and the giant poplars outside. I followed the bold lines of his shadowy profile in the afternoon light, grabbed my pen and readied myself, and then he began to dictate:

Memorandum. When I was still a young medical student, merely aspiring, it fell to the class to carry out an autopsy on a woman taken by a particularly acute case of tetanus. The woman was a member of the local hoi polloi, and her body, in the most unpleasant way, had stiffened into an arc due to cramp. We had had to pry loose the peasant's stiff arms in order to reach the abdomen, which was swollen with hunger and from which we hoped to remove at least some of the internal organs. Her bosom was ample, and the two long teats kept drooping this way or that as we toiled with the cadaver, making a generally hideous impression. When by chance I allowed my eyes to rest on the deceased's face, it was as if the room began to quake. In that moment, our tugging and pushing caused the thin lips of the mouth to part, and an inky darkness was suddenly revealed, from which I could not tear my eyes. It was as if I had peered right into eternity and there was an abyss that wished to devour me. Even as I walked back home through the lanes that afternoon, I could not shake this impression, along with the gruesome sensation, and the sky above me was like a sil-ver-grey dome weighing on my young head. In the evening, a ball was being hosted, not among the grander ones, which I attended, in the company of my fellow students, with heavy steps. It was at a time when I would often sit in my chamber, absorbed in my studies or reading poetry, if not penning a few mournful verses of my own. Ever since I was a young lad, I'd been given to acute shyness when in any form of contact with the opposite sex; I found no pleasure in balls and events or in visits to brothels, which my fellow students insisted upon; often I paid the girl the moment I entered the room and then went home with my business unfinished. At parties and dances, I might observe my companions' frank conversations with the ladies with whom they were acquainted, night-eyed creatures and coquettes who my contemporaries approached like tomcats who'd been basking in the sun: I myself suffered from a tied tongue, or entered into peculiar quarrels in my attempts to converse with women, especially if the snaps had gone to my head or the young lady herself had a sharp tongue. On the evening in question, how-ever, I gathered my courage and asked one of the visiting girls to waltz; the girl was ordinary enough and so unable to refuse me.

She smelled of gingerbread and something else, a staleness, but it was pleasant enough at first. Then, in the middle of the dance, the feeling from earlier in the day suddenly returned, along with the image of the dead woman's maw, and when, after the last notes of the waltz rang out, the girl I was dancing with leaned forward to say something, her mouth half-open, I was overcome with horror and had to dash off. On that night, and many nights thereafter, I had a recurring dream: I turn the abysmal face away from me and lower the dissecting knife I have raised in order to make my first incision across the peasant's belly, and then I pluck the woman's womb from that opening and weigh it in my hands—

One day, Master Valdemar himself was sitting at the square piano when I came into the drawing-room. He wasn't playing. His hair curled at the nape; it had grown long and untidy after all his days and nights in the library. He had a half-drunk cup of punch on the piano lid. His back to the light. Through the drawing-room window in the afternoon dark, I could see that out on the field the hares, still white and luminous after the winter, were fleeing toward the forest's edge. *Won't you come in,* said Master Valdemar without turning around. *Perhaps you'll play a bit for me.* Outside, the field was still and flecked with grey, the snow almost gone now; I stood in the doorway in my stockinged feet, the toes sopping from my aimless garden games. I curtsied, though the master couldn't see me. Then he rose from the stool and turned to me; he was wearing the doctor's smoking jacket and a pair of old, untied boots; inside the shoes he was barefoot. His green smile flashed in the strip of light that fell from the ceiling sconces as he stepped aside and gestured toward the piano with his hand. *I can tell you want to,* he said, and, with the other hand, he snatched the half-drunk glass from the lid. I hesitated before walking the few steps through the drawing-room to the stool. I didn't look at the master as I took my seat; on the music stand was one of Fanny's cheap scores from the city: a polka. I kept my eyes on the field outside as the afternoon dark rolled in, I placed my fingers on the keys, the piano clanged as foully as before. After the final notes, at first there was utter silence. Then the curly-locked man began to applaud: six or seven slow, lingering claps. When I glanced to the side, where the sound was coming from, I saw him on the sofa, where he lay with his undone boots atop the velvet, Fanny's embroidered pillow tucked behind his neck. *You're quick on the keys,* he said in that light, curious voice. I stood up and curtsied once more before walking out of the room and into the hallway to the kitchen and up the stairs to my nursery. As I left, I avoided exchanging looks with the eyes on the sofa. The smell of egg soup wafted through the house. The blackbird sang in the rowan tree outside the nursery window, though the field was already black and invisible in the darkness below. I slept with the bandage on; I dreamed of the black flower from before, of it crumbling again and again, smearing across my fingers.

At dawn I sat on the kitchen steps with the whittling knife and a piece of damp bark while Krantz hitched the horse to the carriage and went into town; when he came back in the afternoon, Doctor Eldh was with him. I was standing in front of Krantz's shard of mirror in the barn and heard the horse squelching into the courtyard, through the mud that had been exposed underneath the snow, and the creaking of the carriage wheels. The filth was ingrained at my hairline and my cheeks were hollow and grey from the winter; I had grown tall and had to adjust the shard to see my face. I spat on my skirt and carved the dirt out of my ears with the fabric. A bare ribbon of light quaked at the edge of the evening sky. Fanny was waiting by the tub in the kitchen; she'd laid out the half-silk dress on the bench next to it, and clean pantalettes;

the doctor had already got out of the carriage and was sitting in the drawing-room with the curly-locked man. Fanny left me alone to wash; she'd hung the blanket over the kitchen window, sent Hulda and Gustava out, and she herself stood folding linens in the corridor outside. I peeled the clothes and bandage off my body, I climbed into the tub, I ran the brush over my arms and legs. Not touching the slit or the boils. I rubbed my hairline. Behind the wall, I could hear the doctor and the master carousing while I dried myself with the flannel and slid my legs into the pantalettes, then I laced up the bodice and stepped into the dress. The sleeves were too short now and I had to blow all the air out of my lungs to fasten every button; I combed and braided my wet hair myself. I fastened the loop braids with the yellow bows that Fanny had laid out. Then I sat down to wait on the long bench until I was called in.

The doctor stayed at Lilltuna for seven days. He walked along the drystone wall with Master Valdemar in a twilight that made the house's plaster exterior walls sparkle like red gold; he sat in the drawing-room and smoked and talked and drank the punch or sloeberry wine that Fanny fetched from the food cellar. In the evenings, I was called to the square piano and I took the stool: it was pitch dark outside, and I could see the outline of my reflection in the pane before me. Toward the centre of the glass, the faces of the doctor and the curly-locked man hung like two floating ovals behind me, glaring and lit up by the shine of the crystal chandelier, my own backlit face dark and indistinct. The first evening, I played a short march, the notes clanging awfully, but behind me on the drawing-room sofa sat Master Valdemar, offering as brief an applause as before. He smiled and squinted with his emerald smile when I turned around to curtsy. When the doctor asked if the master might possibly consider applying his expertise to the instrument, perhaps going so far as to tune it, the man declined, saying he had to be careful with his aching hands after the cold and torturous winter. *Naturally,* said the doctor. *And now see to it that you rest well and properly out here, so your health can be restored, and do allow the country air to reinvigorate you for as long as you deem necessary.*

The curly-locked man sipped the sloeberry wine, his eyelids half-shut, and I noticed that his Cupid's bow was sharp where it curved under his pale moustache, like a carefully drawn pencil mark.

The next morning the doctor sent Krantz to fetch the piano tuner. I waited up in my nursery in my sailor costume, its side seams creaking.

After the tuner had been driven home, once I'd heard him sitting and clinking and tightening the instrument downstairs, a little present lay in a gift box outside my door. In the box were two blood-red silk ribbons. When I was summoned in the evening, I fastened them tightly to my head by the roots of each braid, I pinched my cheeks for colour, I went down to the square piano. As I entered, the doctor was sitting on the sofa with his waistcoat unbuttoned, next to Master Valdemar. Who looked up at me with that veiled, sloe-eyed gaze.

I looked for an anchor point out in the dark field again, marked the silence; I let my fingers run lightly and freely across the instrument as I played the doctor's favourite songs from Fanny's sheet music. The notes were now bright and soft, and the piano no longer jangled. Afterwards, from the sofa, the doctor and the master applauded for a long time, and my eyes searched the black reflection with its tight braids in the window before me: the girl's face in there was smooth and dark, as if it had been erased and replaced by something, I couldn't think of what. The sound of the doctor's big hands slapping and smacking each other enthusiastically sent tingles through my limbs. I was still Incurable; I rose from the screw stool and curtsied. Then I saw that Master Valdemar was still wearing the doctor's smoking jacket, though his boots were now tied. Out in the kitchen hallway, the number of empty bottles grew, their bottoms black and clotted with berry sludge.

I noticed that the master was easily distracted as he conversed with the doctor on the sofa under the crystal chandelier, from time to time seeming to fall into his own thoughts or to lose interest; these shifts in the master caused the doctor to tremble behind his pince-nez, and he would search the other's face uncertainly, and his manner of speech would become urgent and submissive, as if to draw the master back into the conversation. I thought of those invisible people the doctor sometimes addressed in the library during my lessons, how he hissed curses at covert enemies who at once seemed to surround him: Master Valdemar was not among them. During those days, when the door of the library was ajar, and the doctor and the master were walking the grounds, I would peer into the darkness of the room. The walnut table was cluttered with papers and strange equipment, and placed on the clutter was the master's shiny topper. In the shadows, the clock ticked on the wall, the gilded leaves on its case glinting faintly in the light from outside.

Occasionally, I sat up in my window, fixing my eyes on Doctor Eldh down there as he walked with Master Valdemar in the pasture. The doctor wore his winter coat over his cardigan, and a cloud of pipe smoke encircled him, rising and billowing into the sky. On a few occasions they stopped to press their foreheads together, like father and son or two mourners, before proceeding in the dusk. From my distance I tried to make out their faces as they walked by the dry-stone wall, how they were drawn to each other and lit up so strangely in one another's company. I thought of how, during our excursions around Lilltuna, the doctor had walked with me along the ditches and looked at the flowers in the meadows: the memory of his big dry hand fluttered behind my forehead, like a last summer butterfly.

When it was time for supper, Hulda went to call the doctor and the master inside. I watched her dart to the edge of the garden and stand there, putting it on and currying favour and curtsying to the master: she'd neglected to put her cap on her head, and the March wind teased the strands around her braided bun.

The master's pensive gaze lingered on her; he puffed his pipe.

The rowan creaking in the wind. The floor gently groaning.

Soon after the black-haired sisters were taken from me, I was woken up onc dawn by Fanny, standing over my bed with her shawl wrapped around her head and her overcoat on. I sat up and let her dress me; I asked no questions, and she stayed silent, with an odd and somewhat dissolved expression on her face. She put me in my wool skirt and blouse, she laced my boots tightly and carefully, and then she lifted me from the bed and carried me through the house before setting me down in the courtyard and taking me by the hand. She began to walk with me across the field toward the main road. When we reached the crest of the hill, she came to a stop, and pulled a small bundle from her shawl and pressed it into my arms: the bundle smelled freshly baked, and I felt the rough edges of a loaf under the fabric. It was getting brighter. In a farmhouse further off, the candles in the windows were lit, and they burned, and Fanny looked at me with that dissolved face before she turned on her heel and headed back toward Lilltuna. I stood on the crest of the hill with the neighbouring farm behind me, hearing the distant barking of dogs and a door slam and echo across the hills as I watched Fanny's floating hem as she walked down in the field. Her skirt rose and fell with her steps and was black at the bottom from the dirt, but the fabric above shone chalky-white against the soggy earth. I stood on the crest for a while, then began to run slowly down the field after her. When I caught up with her, she didn't turn around at first but stared straight into the dark, and I could see that she still had that strange face pasted on, like sorrow's grimace: then she pulled the cane from her belt and brandished it at me, driving me back across the field: *You empty-headed creature,* she hissed at me, and: *Go on, run.* Then, louder: *Away with you, idiot child!* And I jumped out of Fanny's way so she wouldn't get me with the cane, but as soon as she started walking again I went after her, and she turned back around and flailed wildly at me, after which I ran away, but each time she started off toward the house I went after her again. At last she sank down in the field at the edge of the garden, her arms hanging limp at her sides in the grey light that expanded through the sky above. I stood a bit away from her, still hugging the bread, and let her sob and sniffle for a while there on the sodden earth, before going over and sitting down with her, and she pulled me into her arms like she had done before, and allowed me to rest with my head nestled by her ribs under her coat. Out of the corner of my eye, I saw Krantz come out and stand at the door of the farmhand's cottage, and he stared before carefully retreating back inside and closing the door and leaving us in peace. *Foolish girl,* she whispered, and kept stroking my hair, until at last we got up and went inside, and Fanny sat me down on the long bench in the kitchen while she lit the stove and started clattering with the kettles as usual. I unwrapped the bread from the cloth and tore the hard crust in two and picked at the fresh white interior as the cold left the room. Outside, the sun's flaming red globe pushed its way above Lilltuna.

Drizzle. Straight wet birch trunks. One evening during the spring that Master Valdemar was at Lilltuna, I was summoned to the square piano; Hulda and Gustava and Fanny stood against the drawing-room's long wall. Doctor Eldh looked hunched and uncomfortable on the sofa; it was clear the idea had not been his. Master Valdemar smiled broadly as he leaned an elbow on the square piano. *Come now, enter,* he said, raising his glass with his other hand as if in a toast. *Miss Caesaria, don't you know that music is meant to have an audience?* Doctor Eldh was still fidgeting on the sofa, but he nodded and hummed in approval, his smile strained. Fanny had lit the candles in the sconces, and it was hot and stuffy in the drawing-room. I could see that Hulda had smoothened her hair at her forehead and her parting glistened from water or grease; her face looked ruddy, like she might have pinched her cheeks, and she'd removed her apron and was standing in only her woollen dress next to Gustava.

I sat down at the square piano and played the doctor's favourites from the sheet music, stretching the notes and letting them become new and surprising. When I turned around again, I saw Hulda blushing by the wall, eyes fixed on the curly-locked man. Fanny and Gustava were both staring at the floor. The curly-locked man stood in the middle of the room, feigning applause, one long, claw-like hand against the back of the other, which was still holding the glass.

During that time, Doctor Eldh did not ask me into the library to practise dictation; he brought no toys with him. At night I dreamed again of the deserted house, the flower that over and again turned to ash in my hands. The little black petals always looked ancient, and I only had to touch them lightly for them to fall apart.

April now.

Birds streaking across the white dome of sky.

In the library downstairs, after visiting with the doctor in the drawing-room, Master Valdemar plodded around in his boots well into the small hours. I lay down on the floor of the nursery in my nightclothes; sometimes I pressed my ear to the floor tiles, and the clinking of glass and the noise of the master colliding with the furniture downstairs went straight into my skull. Then the creatures would loosen themselves from the room's shadowy corners, as if they'd begun to spill from my sleep into waking, and I'd squeeze my eyes shut until tears came to hold the boundary of the dream. And the black velvet came from the nursery's darkened corners, and careened and was torn in two, and the cut-outs appeared and pressed their long limbs against me until I had to sit up and violently shake them off. Outside, the nights were brighter now; they arrived slowly and relentlessly and settled upon the house like a damp blanket after the first crack of twilight, like an eggshell from which seeps a rosy light. Soft rain at eventide swallowed then by darkness.

The evening before the doctor left, spirits down in the drawing-room were high. Through the floorboards I could hear him talking to Master Valdemar, though as if through a tin can: the words blurred and lost their edges, and only when night came did the voices fade and fall silent, replaced by the doctor's creaking sounds from the drawing-room sofa, where he must have drifted off. At first the house was still. But after a while an unfamiliar rustling reached me from down by the rowan outside my window, and I sat up in the darkness of the nursery. Then, at once, Hulda's birdlike voice rang out into the night, followed by another voice, more muffled and laconic, strange until I recognized it. At first there was chirping down there, as there always was when Hulda was in such a humour, but then a new tone entered the warbling: there was a pressing at first, or a feeble pleading, then sobbing and whimpering, and then the jostling became more intense, and it began to thud and rub and scrape down there against the outer wall. I walked up to the window in my stockinged feet and pressed my face to the pane, tilting my head to look at the wall: it was dark there under the rowan tree. The sky above was grey as midnight approached, but when the little body suddenly detached itself from the wall, there was still enough light to make out that striped woollen dress darting across the courtyard, toward the garden. The head and hands weren't visible, only the dress, which flickered as the curly-locked man chased Hulda between the poplars. Her warbling voice continued to beg and plead as she ran. I could vaguely discern the master's pale curls and his dark, slender hands at last catching hold of Hulda by the striped wool, after which the dress was wrenched onto the wet earth and became more and more dirty and difficult to distinguish while, lying on the ground, Hulda was dragged back to the wall, under the rowan, and disappeared. And the voice stopped its pleading, as the scraping and thudding against the wall began again, and grew louder, before a sudden silence. I withdrew, and for a while nothing could be heard down there except for the jangle of a buckle or belt. Then I heard the curly-locked man squelch back to the house in the mud, and the kitchen door opened and shut behind him.

The doctor was snoring in the drawing-room. The master's boots creaked as he walked through the house and into the library, where he moved around for a while before more silence. Under the rowan by the wall, not a sound. A fresh rain fell.

In the morning, Hulda sat in the kitchen next to Gustava and ate her gruel with her cap tied securely under her chin. And when Gustava playfully kicked Hulda's toes under the table, as she usually did, Hulda didn't kick back: she just stared into her gruel. Her face looked grey and strange. No sneering smile; no eyes rolling with unattainable freedom like they had that time among the raspberries. I noticed that she left her cap on when, later in the day, on Fanny's orders, she went to call the master and the doctor to the table. I sat on the bench under the glass roof of the veranda, gnawing on a winter apple, and watched her as she walked in a slow arc across the courtyard. Her braided bun was tucked into her cap, and she stopped at the foot of the gazebo, where the doctor and the master sat talking and smoking, but she did not enter. I could see the curly-locked man's face through the glass, how it shone and magnified in the flicker of the lantern they'd taken out with them. Further inside, the doctor's big hands stuck out at me, though his face was hidden as he scraped his pipe. Hulda curtsied at the foot of the gazebo steps, forearms tucked under her apron. She uttered Mam'selle Fanny's message about the meal. She didn't lift her gaze. Her cheeks were colourless in the grainy midday light. Spring was near.

Later that day I stood with Fanny on the front steps and watched the doctor's carriage disappear over the crest of the hill. And, again, Master Valdemar asked for his meal to be served on the tray inside the library. For the next few days he dined with the door closed before opening it, in the same way each time, to slide the tray in an arc across the floor before shutting it again. I avoided the square piano; in the daytime I sat in my nursery and drew horses on the slate that Doctor Eldh had given me for my birthday.

But, come each evening, the thudding below the rowan tree would resume. And no warbling sounded, and no woollen dress darted among the trees. There was only Hulda's feeble pleading, briefly, and then the shushing and scraping and the dull thuds against the wall, as from the back of a head or an elbow, and then the silence again, and the jangling belt, followed by the squelching toward the house and the kitchen door being opened and shut. And every morning, Hulda sat grey and indisposed with her gruel, while Gustava cast anxious glances at her across the table, and Fanny stood, her back tense, facing the kettle, its steam billowing around her. Outside, Krantz took longer and longer walks into the pasture; he ran unnecessary errands to the woodshed, and slipped out to the animals, and did not come in for gruel.

The black furrow at the edge of the field smeared my boots with soil.

I returned the sailor costume and the silk dress to the wardrobe, and bandaged myself.

Once when I came in from the garden at dusk, Master Valdemar sat wrapped up in the garden armchair, muttering and grumbling in his particular way. He'd stuck his glass bottle in the grass at arm's reach; the evening sun flashed against it, its rosy light giving one last spark from above the pines. As darkness fell, Gustava went out with the lantern and replaced the empty bottle with one that was full, wearing clogs and a winter shawl though it had warmed up. Blackbirds. Now and again, the master fell asleep out there, and Krantz had to prise him away and help him to bed. I would sit, unseen, in the darkened drawing-room, listening to Krantz stagger along the corridor under Master Valdemar's full weight, before they reached the master's room and Krantz got him through the door. The green square of light would strike the floor, and I could see that inside the writing stool was overturned, and the master's gaiters had been hung to dry over the arm of the doctor's chair: they looked stiff and forlorn. The wall clock was silent again, the master had stopped winding it: I avoided the black eye in the centre of its face. Then the door was pulled shut.

WHEN THE BLACK-HAIRED SISTERS still lived at Lilltuna, I often played in the corridor outside the kitchen, waiting for them to finish their chores and have a moment's rest; then I would run out and sit on the hill with them for a while, as they chewed on whatever bread Fanny had given them. The sun would slide out of the clouds and glitter in their black braids. One of the sisters had a small scar at the corner of her mouth, which is how Fanny would come to distinguish one from the other when they persisted in switching their pinafores. As for me, I knew who was who, even from a distance, as they would walk toward me from the barns or the pasture with their particular limping gait; I sensed the small differences in their laughter, in the smell of their hair.

In my dream they're standing on the far side of the pond.

The girls who were brought to Lilltuna over the years were always scrawny and slovenly when they arrived, but after a few days they'd usually fatten up. Had I stayed in the city when I was born, I might have been given a name like one of theirs. Fredrika or Hanna, Valborg or Josefina. Once they'd arrived, they would sit on the long kitchen bench with their shawls on and gobble up the meat gravy and Fanny's rusks: afterwards, they found it hard to keep their eyes open, and their faces burned with intense satisfaction.

Only the scrawniest and most slovenly girls from the city could be enticed to work at Lilltuna, with me present, under Fanny: that much was clear. They came with Krantz in the horse-drawn carriage or with Doctor Eldh in the cabs with their hired coachmen: they always had bad teeth, and skirts and work blouses that were too big or too small, and they were filthy, and laconic, or else chattered more than Fanny liked, and the food in the first few days always made them giddy, not to mention the stomach gripes that followed. If they were in too sorry a state, they wouldn't last long at Lilltuna, and they mustn't be gossipmongers or too simple of mind: they had to behave themselves and be patient in their work and not ask too many questions.

I suppose Doctor Eldh thought that nothing would ever change out at Lilltuna, and nor did it. People rarely came by, just the piano tuner and the farmer with the yearlings. Occasionally, chaises and carriages clattered by beyond the boundary hedge, and only once, one autumn, did a wagon lose its way and stray toward the house.

When it happened, the vehicle was filled with a flock of schoolchildren; Fanny had noticed too late. Not even Krantz, who was far away in the pasture when the wagon rolled into the courtyard, had time to divert it. Fanny immediately sent me up to the nursery and locked me in, and I watched her from the window as she wiped her hands on her apron while taking her place on the front steps. It was during this same autumn that the black-haired sisters were driven to the city by Krantz, never to return, and the doctor still hadn't found any new maids to assist Fanny, and only she and Krantz and I were left at Lilltuna.

Sat on the box, next to the young coachman holding the reins, was a schoolmarm in a blue velvet blouse and jacket: she smiled broadly at Fanny as the wagon slowed to a stop, and fiery tendrils blew from the big loose chignon she had made with the swell of her hair and pinned at the crown of her head. The jacket's velvet and its small black buttons gleamed across the woman's chest in the early autumn glow, and the children had already begun climbing out and hopping onto the gravel like a swarm of grasshoppers, though Fanny raised her hands defensively and slid her anxious eyes to the window, where I was hiding behind the lace curtain. The children were of various sizes, and wore shoes and striped cotton dresses, and had schoolbooks strapped together with worn leather belts, and some had loop braids, like me, but they were looser and more tousled and not tied with silk bows. Their faces were still tanned from the summer and freckled, and their eyes were bold and quick; from my hiding place, I imagined the colours of the girls' lively eyes—brown, grey-green, sea blue, and yellow.

I had to sit up in the nursery all day because something was wrong with the wagon's wheels, and Krantz had to help the young coachman knock and prod the spokes while the children roamed Lilltuna in alarming patterns in the pale daylight. They sat on the gate to the pasture and fed straw and flowers to the cows; they drew figures and eerie animals in the mud by the front steps; they tossed apples between them and pulled at one another's hair, and they ran straight out under the canopy of trees in the garden in their dusty boots. Fanny went in and out of the house with coffee for the schoolmarm and the coachman and apples for the children; she did not invite them inside to warm up and she did not let anyone out of her sight. Afternoon came. Hunger tore at my stomach, and my mouth was rough and tart with thirst. But at last Krantz and the coachman finished with the wheels and it was time for the group to depart. In the darkening afternoon, I saw the schoolmarm give Fanny a long, curious look as she and Krantz practically shoved her and the coachman onto the box. The schoolmarm furrowed her brow and let her gaze drift across the house, and her flickering fire-hair was a small halo framing her round face with its kindly, watchful eyes, and behind her the children climbed onto the wagon and sat down and jostled for space, and I retreated further into the room behind the curtain while the coachman smacked the horses and the vehicle drove off.

The September evening.

It was shortly after the schoolchildren had been at Lilltuna that Fanny had pulled me from my bed, there in the dawn, and planted me on the crest of the hill with the freshly baked bread in my arms.

I sat in the locked nursery and looked out at the children, who ran and played downstairs with their dresses and books and water-bright eyes.

I stood on the crest of the hill in the dawn mist, squeezing the loaf in my arms. Then I ran back down the field, back to Lilltuna.

May came. Fanny continued to pass through the hallway with Master Valdemar's meals. Increasingly the food would be untouched when she returned, but the glass would always be empty. The doctor was keeping to the city again; at dusk the clouds sailed with unnatural leisure across the sky, flesh-coloured and illuminated from below by a solar shimmer. My forearms got stung by the nettles as I walked through the garden. The mosquitoes came, and the rancid scent of rowan blooms reached me through my nursery window along with the marshy smell of the fields that lay beyond.

At suppertimes, Hulda sat opposite me over the veal soup, flakes of fat coating its surface like fallen pine needles on a swamp. Her eyelids were always lowered, her face still slicked with grey. She twitched at every sound that came from the library. Had stopped warbling. *Hulda, dear,* Gustava pleaded in a low voice when Fanny was out of earshot, but Hulda didn't answer: she simply turned further inward, toward the grey, and every time her toes were kicked under the table, she drew her feet close to her. From time to time she'd give Gustava a strained smile across the table, as if to offer her comfort, but the smile was dull and faint, and I noticed the storm behind her eyes, and I thought of the woollen dress flickering and zigzagging between the trees before it was chased down, and pulled back to the wall through the wet earth, and torn. *Come now, Gustava, it's nothing,* Hulda would say through her grey smile. Then Gustava would sob in despair, and her pockmarked face would contort for a few seconds over the gruel.

Mornings arriving in a narrow strip above the forest's contours. The yellow daylight breaking through and causing the dewy field to glisten. The scent of spring rising from the fields. I no longer did my sums in the doctor's notebooks. I did not open the *Flora*.

One day, when I was sitting idly in my nursery, fussing with the toys that had started to look worn and lustreless, there was a sudden thunder of footsteps up the stairs, and the door was thrown open and the curly-locked man appeared in my doorway. I knew at once that it was him, though I hardly recognized him: he'd taken the old knight's helmet and cuirass that had belonged to Lilltuna's previous owner from the cupboard downstairs and made a fright of himself. Under the cuirass he wore the doctor's smoking jacket, but there was nothing on his feet; the nails on his slender, finger-like toes were untrimmed. Between the visor and the beaver, a tuft of his beard jutted out, now grown long; it drew back into the helmet, and I imagined the face behind the metal breaking into a smile.

The curly-locked man stood motionless for a moment in his bare feet, heavy on the threshold; I could see his eyes gleaming through the visor and I sat frozen on the floor, among the scattered toys. *Well, look who's having a grand time,* he said suddenly from within the helmet, his voice breathless and trapped. His slender fingers ran along the edges of the cuirass. *Miss Caesaria does indeed have a grand time out here,* he repeated.

I was incapable of rising from the floor; in my hand I still held a blue velvet sofa from the dollhouse. Spring birds in the trees outside. The curly-locked man took a step backwards, out of the room, gave me one last look through the armour, then pushed the door shut. The muted, lingering thuds down the stairs.

I waited in the nursery until I heard Fanny in the corridor downstairs, the serving dish clinking on the tray; then I went out to the barn, and I picked up one of Krantz's old shovels that was leaning against the wall and I broke off the tip—I left the handle on the shaft. Out in the pasture, Krantz was walking among the dairy—I could see as much through the grimy barn window. When he was far enough away, I went into the farmhand's cottage and dug out the discarded wadmal trousers that had been lying unused in the entryway under the boards and scrap.

And with this, I had the trousers and the golden Sceptre with which to cast off the Beast of Fire.

AFTER THAT MORNING, WHEN I was a small child and Fanny had planted me on the crest of the hill, she began to leash me less and less often. I'd sometimes go to her myself with the rope in hand; I'd become accustomed to having it drag behind me as I played in the garden or ran between the barns. She'd look at me with her weary eyes and take the rope from my hand and put it round my waist, tying two extra knots so it wouldn't come loose as I played. I built huts of twigs and brushwood under the gnarliest of the fruit trees; I lined up the horse and tin soldiers by the hedge. Before darkness fell, I simply wound the rope around my wrist and went back to the house.

Cloud-streak. Wind shaking the linden crowns. Flower-burst.

When the black-haired sisters were still working for Fanny and had not yet been sent away from Lilltuna, they would sometimes come to my nursery with various finds after accompanying Krantz to the city. They'd each give me a secretive look and pull item after item from their shawls and apron pockets, all stolen when Krantz wasn't looking: half-eaten sugar buns and small soft plums that we shared under the trees in the garden, out of Fanny's sight; tin spoons we bent into funny figures; a single cracked glasses lens fallen from its frame. Once they brought a stack of newspapers and handed them to me, eyes twinkling in anticipation, and they sat on the ground and leaned against the trunk of one of the grey pear trees in the garden while I sounded my way through column after column of notices, advertisements, and articles, reading aloud as they gnawed on unripe fruit they'd snatched from the tree. The sharp spring sun fell through the tangles of branches overhead and burned the bridges of our noses, but it didn't matter, and I read about steamships and bank offices and photography studios and operettas performed at the city theatre: about the dance school, the boy's academy, and the evening school for maids. I read about the distribution of alms to beggars at the police station, and the property auctions, and the masquerade ball held in the spring and the children's ball held during the city feast in honour of the Annunciation. I read the *For Sale* section announcing the sale of oats, rye, and timothy seeds, of hat liners, suitcases, half-wool fabrics, and items made of tin plate, of window frames and woollen yarns and oranges and velocipedes, and the city with its hustle and bustle bounced and burned behind my forehead as I sat with the pages open there, next to the black-haired sisters, under the pear tree. All the while I was thinking of Doctor Eldh, and of his daughters at his city residence, and the maids who dressed the girls in the mornings, and combed their hair, and how they sat, properly dressed, with their tutors in their rooms during lessons. And that one of the daughters might yawn and sleepily blink in the daylight falling through the windows, while the rattle of cabs and the clatter of hooves came in from outside, and bobbing into the window frame perhaps were the tops of hats and umbrellas going past, all under the sky that appeared above the roof ridges. And it all seemed so wondrous as I read aloud, and my thoughts and images of the city grew and turned golden and expanded in my head as the black-haired sisters encouraged me, gnawing on grey pears. But then, in the midst of my reading, there might arise a painful and peculiar note, and all at once the images would become distorted and threatening and blurred, and the doctor's words about the darkness would come to mind, the things he said about the wretched cold, and the pits of the earth, and the children playing in that other world, the world I'd never seen, as if it lay at the edge of a great and wicked sleep. And the black-haired sisters would give me a curious look, each with a sharp, girlish face, and their skirts would glitter in the sun falling through the branches overhead, and, afterwards, they'd get gripes from all the pears.

Even after the black-haired sisters had left Lilltuna, I would, when alone, take out the cracked newspapers from the places I'd hid them in the nursery; I'd read them at dawn, in the trembling light of the tallow candle stump I kept next to the bed. And again the images and the smells and the sounds and the shimmer-sky above the city roofs would loom, and I didn't know if all that arose from those pages made me frightened, or wistful.

LITTLE BEDA ARRIVED ONE evening in early spring, with Krantz in the carriage from the city, sat behind some baskets. I saw her head was uncovered and a woollen shawl was wrapped around her shoulders; you could tell from afar there was something not quite right about her. Her hair was braided but the braids seemed to have been slept on for a long time; tousled and irregular, they came flying over her shoulders when the carriage lurched to a stop near the kitchen steps.

I stood at my nursery window, the doctor had left again, and behind the lace curtain I held tight to the broken-off shovel with the fingers of one hand. I watched Fanny come out, her cardigan pulled around her shoulders, to receive the new girl. I assumed she'd been brought here at the doctor's request and to replace Hulda, whose pace had slowed and who now sat over her gruel with that strange face, or was it just to bolster the household now that Master Valdemar needed so much looking after?

The May sky was sheer and pale blue, and I could see that the new girl had a gnarled and uneven face, and that her upper lip was split up to her nose. Under her mousy hair, which was styled in a sloppy parting, her scalp shone with grease and filth. She was tall, too, and her posture was hunched, but her movements were careful and her gait brisk as she got out of the carriage and followed Fanny up the kitchen stairs and into the house.

At supper she sat opposite me in the kitchen, next to Hulda, who had not yet been driven away from Lilltuna;

I never asked Fanny about the maids who came and went over the years or what her plans were for them. The new girl, eyes lowered, gulped down the potato soup; her cleft lip caused an ugly slurp, and I could see that several teeth were missing in there: she looked childlike under the grime but might have been a couple of years older than I was. *Won't you introduce yourself to the others?* Fanny suddenly and sharply asked from across the table. There was a moment's silence and the new girl halted her soup spoon. Then she pulled a piece of crumpled paper from her shawl and flattened it against the tabletop with one hand. She pushed the paper across the wood to Fanny, who stared at it, and at the large angular letters written on it. *Caesaria?* she commanded after a moment's hesitation, and I craned my neck and read from my seat; the letters were difficult to decipher through the many folds that made the paper shadowed and angled in the faint glow of the tallow candle. *Beda Sköld,* I read aloud at last, and then the new girl muttered something barely audible through that cleft lip, and I could see that her eyes were brown and shy, one with the suggestion of a squint. *Little Beda?* Gustava asked, then the girl nodded and reached for the note and tucked it back into her shawl. And she resumed slurping down her soup.

After that she was left on her own, to drag in from the barn the straw mattress that Krantz slept on in the winter, and to put it, on Fanny's orders, on the floor of the maid's room where Hulda and Gustava's sofa had been returned for the spring. And at dawn the new girl went with the others and Krantz to milk the cows. I sat at the nursery window, wide awake, and recited the words of Jesus to drive away the shadows in the room. I rolled the shovel between my palms. Then the sun's orb pushed up above the treetops in the forest behind the field, and day broke.

142

In the evenings, Master Valdemar would again sit in the garden armchair, drinking, or he'd sleep in the library under the wall clock. When he was in the armchair with his bottle, he seemed to take no notice of the new girl. If he became sufficiently drowsy from the drink and sleep took him, the wall under the rowan would stay silent at night, and there would be no scraping or thudding. And yet Gustava would cast her questioning glances at Hulda across the morning gruel. Hulda still had her grey face, flinching at each sound that came from the library: an object falling to the floor, plodding steps across the tiles. Fanny stood with the kettles, her back turned to us, and Krantz kept to the animals outside, or he chopped wood up on the hill, taking long pauses between each chop, as if hesitant.

The evenings warmed and reached into the nights.

In the mornings, I opened the nursery window and let in the early-summer scents—dung and nectar, meadow grass. Below, Krantz would carry two enamel buckets filled with rainwater, to rinse the aisle between the animals in the barn. Master Valdemar did not leave the library for days on end. The sky was an unbroken sheet of blue. I'd begun to walk barefoot in my clogs, and, when the sun was shining, I stepped out of them and stood on the grass at the end of the garden with my face turned to the sky; the sun was bright and burned my cheeks and forehead, and time would spin and stand still, or there'd be no time, only the eternity of summer, stretching across the rolling landscape with its acreages and roads, making the rising forest sweat out its queasy smell of needles and sour earth. Cabbage-white butterflies flitting through the grass between the trees' twisted trunks.

When I returned from my aimless excursions in the garden, the new girl would be sitting on the hill and rinsing potatoes, or shaking the soil off the turnips in the tub beside her. She worked efficiently and needed little admonition but

143

rarely responded with more than a mumble when addressed. When words did press out of her, a faint whistling came from her cleft mouth. And the milking was done quickly now that Krantz had three helpers.

The doctor came back from the city one evening in June, he arrived suddenly and without warning. He had with him a new hired coachman, who Krantz showed to the guest cubby in the farmhand's cottage, and he had his walking stick, one with a lion's head that he usually took on our excursions in the meadows around Lilltuna. I hadn't had time to wash, but Fanny gave me a quick scrub with a rag in the darkness behind the door before we stepped out; she had me put my dirty feet in boots that she hastily laced in the entryway. Her movements were brisk and urgent, and then she rose up and opened the door and pushed me out into the evening light to receive the doctor. He'd flattened his top hat and was clutching it under his arm as he went up the stairs.

He seemed in good cheer, he asked for evening punch with his coffee on the glass veranda. Fanny immediately drew my bath, and I carefully scrubbed my body with the brush behind the kitchen curtains. The boils' growth had stemmed somewhat, but they looked miserable when I took off the bandage, flattened and with bright red lines carved deep into the skin. My arms and legs had grown long and hairy. I dressed and went to the doctor on the veranda. He lit up when he saw me. He patted the cushion on the bench next to him. Out there the evening clouds hung like unmoving flames or torn cotton wool. *Would you play something beautiful?* he said, his large face dimly lit by the dome of twilight above, and I nodded and got up and opened the door so the notes of the square piano would reach him. It was dark in the drawing-room; Fanny had lit the sconces but not the chandelier. The curly-locked man had yet to stir in the library, and the doctor made no effort to summon him.

I sat on the screw stool in the straining sailor costume; the wicked hairs on my arms gleamed below the cuffs of my too-short sleeves, and when the last notes of the piece rang out, I heard crying coming from the veranda. Then I went out to the doctor and sat with him in the darkening night. I lay my hand on his head as he wished. The fireplace crackled in the drawing-room and a shower of sparks flew up as Fanny prodded the wood in the dusk; glowing grasshoppers made of fire whirled around the ash rake. I sat beside the doctor and again listened to the story of my Creation; the sky deepened, and I could hear the voles scurrying under the veranda steps, and the doctor seemed distracted, losing the story's thread several times. The greenery around the gazebo was shadowy and sighing and swallows swirled in the air above and the gooseberries let off their scent, and I knew he was already preparing to leave.

WHEN I THINK OF Doctor Eldh and the man who called himself Master Valdemar, I think of two clouds forming in an otherwise clear evening sky. Coral-red cotton contours. How they recede and then merge, until the one can't be distinguished from the other.

I sat in the cab with the top up and rattled off the names of the flowers; I bent over the walnut table and assembled my times tables with the domed eye of the wall clock watching over me. I was Blessed, then I was Incurable.

The day after the doctor's arrival, Master Valdemar had his hair cut. The doctor went out of the house that day and sat, with his writing instruments and a manuscript, in the gazebo, in only his shirt, no waistcoat, the lion's head cane in his hand and a straw hat on his head. When Master Valdemar emerged, he looked pale and worse for wear; his eyes flitted a bit, but he was obliging as Krantz led him from his bed in the library onto the hill around the back. Then he sat, still and biddable, with a cup of coffee in the garden armchair in the shade under the linden trees while Fanny came out with a washing bowl and a pitcher of water. His pale curls fell into a small pile of glinting gold on the grass behind him as she ran the scissors through his hair; the darker, coarser beard hairs stuck to his woollen trousers, through which you could see the outline of his sharp thighs.

I stood at the corner of the house, watching with my hands tucked into my pinafore. Summer birds. *Thank you, dearest Mam'selle Fanny,* the master said, as she brought out the pocket mirror for him. *You truly are most heartfelt and good to me out here.* Afterwards, he took a long look at his face, angling and turning the little mirror, releasing reflections of light to dance in the lindens overhead, and then, with his dregs of coffee, he went to sit with the doctor, who had gone to the sunshine at the edge of the park. The glossy summer apples hung heavy as fists in the trees; the doctor let me sit in the grass below while they chatted in the blazing sun. Master Valdemar's face looked hollow and pale from his sloeberry slumber and his nightly plodding in the library during the doctor's absence, but he'd twisted his moustache after the haircut, revealing his sharp Cupid's bow, and his freshly shaven chin retained its soft line. His grass-coloured eyes had a dull lustre. I tried to see if the shadow was still lurking somewhere, the unpredictable spot of pitch-black unruly despair behind that smooth forehead that made the master's humours swing and left him cackling in the garden at dusk or jangling his belt in the silence after the warbling stopped under the rowan at night. *Behold, the fairies' arrival,* he said, smiling, when Hulda and Gustava brought out apple turnovers and more coffee, and I caught the hunted glance that grey-faced Hulda gave him before going back into the house, close on Gustava's heels. The doctor cleared his throat and rattled his coffee cup on the saucer. He kept his delighted gaze fixed on the master; he had not yet made any suggestion I be called to my lessons.

Master Valdemar stuck out his little finger as he sat there holding the coffee cup: he had fine, slender fingers and yet they did not resemble pianists' ones—there was something about the little finger, or the languor and fumble of his grip. But perhaps it didn't matter what kind of fingers Master Valdemar had, if they really were as brittle after the winter as he'd described to the doctor. For the doctor lit up so strangely in Master Valdemar's company, listening to his tall tales, and to him grandly holding forth about music, and he somehow came to life. All the while the shadow appeared upon and floated from Master Valdemar's face, in an unpredictable pattern of its own making.

Close stone-grey light. Spatters of gold on the fringes of clouds. Swallows shooting out from between the trees on savage wings.

In the evenings that followed, the doctor and master moved between the drawing-room, the library, and the garden furniture arranged on the grass below the veranda. When I walked on the grass outside the house, I could see them outlined in the green lamplight of the library, the doctor flipping through his manuscripts while the master reclined in the armchair with a thoughtful expression, a cloudy punch cup clasped carefully between the fingertips of both hands, as if he were holding an exotic hummingbird. My wakeful sleep made me sluggish during the day, but in the darkness my vision was keen. At that time, the image of the pond's maw emerged from the night with its shifting stillness and blaze, and it was as if my room had been torn from the rest of the house, floating in its own space; over a vast and peculiar distance, I heard the doctor's and the master's voices downstairs. Strange shapes and faces arose in the nursery, fuzzy and gleaming and smooth as a calf's snout, their eyes always shut on the verge of sleep, and there were grabbing arms, and in fits and starts they whispered inaudible things in insistent voices, as if they wished to tell me something important. Then one of the faces became clearer than the others, and it opened its eyes and looked right at me, and when it did, I knew it was her.

She looked at me questioningly, kindly, with those liquid yellow eyes. And she said, in the Scrawny One's voice: *And*

who has the Sceptre shall quench the fire of the dragon and be
raised to the throne of heaven—

So began her instructions.

THE NEW GIRL LIKED to sit under a linden tree on the hill-side around the back and count pine cones. If no one came out and interrupted her, she could sit there for a long time, her cleft lip muttering and counting as she moved the cones from one side to the other. Spilled light, milky white. The rib cages of giant poplars heaving and sinking in the summer wind. From a distance, as I walked back to the house along the edge of the garden, I could hear the new girl's ramblings as she sat, absorbed in herself, not counting real numbers but ones that seemed to come to her, foreign names she'd spit out with each new cone she placed beside another, there in the grass, before beginning again.

The light shrank with the clouds that crowded above the pine trees. The scent of hawthorn and kerosene. Swarms of gnats above the animals at dusk. On the hottest days, I would lie on the floor up in my nursery; I'd shut my eyes and bathe my face in the sunlight that filtered through the lace curtain, casting roses and white flames this way and that across the room.

The new girl got dressed by herself, and had a hand for plucking chickens, and could braid her own hair with ease but spoke to no one, and she took every opportunity to sit and mutter with the pine cones. She was like a child with the chapped, worn hands of a grown woman: her blouse strained across her chest, and the grime at her hairline was grey even though Fanny had twice gone over her with the brush in the tub; it was as if she had rolled herself in particles of dirt and pitch and could never be made clean. Had the new girl not been so efficient in her work, she wouldn't have lasted long at Lilltuna, but the milking got done and the lambs were fed and the piles of wood inside the shed were straighter than usual. At the kitchen table, Hulda and Gustava sighed as the girl slurped up the food with her cleft lip. Then she'd turn her brown sparkling gaze to me, letting me know that she certainly wasn't going to stop her slurping. The new girl would get restive if something went wrong with her counting, which seemed to forever be going on inside her, a stream of times and objects she gave name to and muttered to herself: if the chunks of wood refused to lie as they should, or if she was interrupted with her cones at the wrong moment, she'd start howling and stomping desperately on the spot while clapping her hands hard and fast, and each time Fanny would come running and give the girl the cane until she was perfectly calm. Then she'd resume her work and chores. And all the while she'd be muttering as she went about her business, as if the counting and organizing formed a protective dome around her. Sometimes I sat on the kitchen steps and poured milk into the saucer for the cat while the new girl was busy with the cones over on the hillside, and I'd listen to her for a while. The afternoon would wring its way through the tree branches and send patches of sun sailing slowly over the grass. And I'd suddenly feel as if I, too, were enclosed in that dome she'd arranged around herself, there in the shell of protective light she fashioned with her words and her rambling, and in there we would come to no harm.

During the summer when Master Valdemar was at Lilltuna, Doctor Eldh visited ever more often. Through the cloud cover, diffuse pillars of light shone, narrow, as if the gaps had been made by an angel's slim finger. Each time the doctor arrived, I waited for him to call me to my lessons, but he only patted me on the head, peering kindly and uncomprehendingly at me when he exited the cab at the front before going to the master, sitting with him in the drawing-room, or outside in the warm evenings. I'd lower my body into the steaming bathing tub, snatches of sky glaring through the tears in the kitchen curtains. The sound of swallows. My hair had grown long; it reached all the way to the small of my back and was dry and tangled at the ends, but Fanny didn't seem to notice: she didn't cut my hair as she'd always done, but rushed between the kitchen and the drawing-room with the trays.

On a few occasions, the doctor brought guests along on his visits, Society fellows and colleagues from the medical faculty: there'd be two or three gentlemen who stuck their heads out of the cab when the coachman jumped down from the box and opened the door. The visitors blinked dizzily at the sun, as if they'd been sitting in an underground burrow or had wriggled out of the ground like earthworms after rain. Yet they arrived as if it were the most natural thing, even though the doctor had never before brought anyone from the city with him out to Lilltuna, except for the maids and the piano tuner and finally Master Valdemar, and a fantasy appeared to me, of Lilltuna's outer edges dissolving and floating off toward what was beyond—the fields and the forest and the farms that became denser, finally transforming into the city. I imagined that the doctor had agreements with the visitors like the one he had with the piano tuner, and I tried to remember the point in time at which he'd stopped feeling the need to shield Lilltuna from the eyes of the world: something must have faded for him, or begun to bore him, like a troublesome haze briskly lifting, dissolving into a clear and ordinary day. Perhaps he simply no longer knew what to make of me. When the food cellar was emptied of Fanny's sloe cordial and punch, the visitors brought their own bottles from the city, drinks of different colours to be sipped in the gazebo in the summer evenings, surrounded by the heady scents of apple and jasmine. As soon as they stepped out of the carriages, the visitors would look at me with interest and a dash of something else, like horror: I'd stand on the front steps in my sailor costume with the far-too-short sleeves, the bodice laced tightly around my belly, and it worried me that Doctor Eldh hadn't noticed how poorly my clothes now fit, that he hadn't brought me new ones, as had been his custom. My waking sleep made my face hollow, I could see as much in Krantz's shard, and my growing arms and legs betrayed my incurable swelling, as did the dog ears inside my bandages that had become increasingly difficult to conceal.

But the doctor didn't seem to take any notice; he called me without a hint of undertone to his voice and asked me to play the songs from the sheet music on the square piano, with the windows open so the music would reach the company that reclined on cushions in the gazebo. At one point, in the middle of a song, I had the uneasy feeling that I'd forgotten how to read music, and everything I'd learned at Lilltuna had vanished as if by a stroke of magic, the times tables and the letters and the names of flowers and everything else the doctor had practised with me in the library under the East Indian wall clock, and I blinked hard until tears fell from the corners of my eyes and ran down my cheeks, and I found my way back to the tempo, following the floating black dots in front of me. Outside, the sound of Krantz splitting wood with his axe resounded. The spruces at the edge of the forest looked like giants with sloping shoulders and severed hands. Master Valdemar buzzed about the visitors, ever attentive and quick to call to Fanny when drinks needed refreshing. She'd go out with the tray, and the master would refill the visitors' half-drunk glasses himself, moving like an obliging and practised host: I might then notice a trembling behind the doctor's pince-nez, as if in mild displeasure, but this would cease as quickly as it had begun. The visitors draped their summer coats over the backs of their chairs and threw their heads back while puffing on their cigars, or fell into laughter at some merriment: sometimes they sat deeply involved in conversations I understood only fragments of, conversations about things that existed beyond Lilltuna, landscapes and phenomena and names I did not know.

From time to time the visitors fell silent and listened intently to the master as he recounted his years at court and his travels on the continent or spoke ardently about music: they smiled along with the indiscretions and sipped their liqueurs with a particular glint in their eyes, and I could never decipher whether that glint expressed unease or enthusiasm. They'd crowd onto the sofa in the drawing-room or into the old, splintering wooden armchairs they'd brought in from the garden, and I'd sit at the square piano to entertain them, the smoke thick behind me, though the windows were wide open to the summer evening. *Hasn't the doctor set up a lovely home here for the girl,* said one of them once when I turned to nod after the recital, then: *The young lady must be glad to have been rescued from her cruel fate, must she not?* And they all turned to me, and after a moment's reflection I said: *Doctor Eldh has been very good to me, having saved me from the city's deafening noise and the cold and darkness of the night by taking me out here to Lilltuna.* There was a hush, and the silence in the room turned slippery and strange as the visitors cast nervous glances at each other before bursting out laughing; I saw a flash from behind the doctor's pince-nez, from unchecked worry or discomfort, and my face felt hot and shapeless. The doctor swallowed hard before joining in the raucous laughter.

The same thing happened between the visitors as happened when the piano tuner called at Lilltuna, and when the doctor walked with Master Valdemar in the pasture: I saw those invisible threads and connections moving through the air; looks and expressions that interjected the words that drifted from one person to the next: greedy, provocative flutters, unspoken questions and answers, equally tangible and intangible. It was as if the guests were speaking a language I didn't understand but was nonetheless always scanning, and I adapted my movements to its patterns, its grammar, and if I accidentally broke its rules my face dissolved, annihilated by heat. Because the visitors kept returning, I learned that grammar, in the same way I'd learned everything else out at Lilltuna: the deepening irregularities of the floor tiles; the rays of light across the sheet of sky that turned into dark night; the burrows in the ground the animals left behind under the spruce trees.

Master Valdemar smiled with his lips closed: the smile made his twisted moustache point sideways above the sharp contour of his upper lip, giving him a feline look. I curtsied deeply and wished the visitors a good night, then walked through the illuminated drawing-room with the master's grass-coloured eyes stinging the back of my neck, and into the hallway and up the stairs to my nursery. My waking sleep was like a blanket of fur around me, and the nursery loosened its joints and floated away in the night. Slow rectangles of July's gauzy light swept across the floor tiles.

I walked barefoot in the garden between the fruit trees; I looked at the dead magpie chicks that had fallen from their nests and were now smeared on the ground. Their eye sockets were empty and some of their beaks broken, the wings barely visible and half-melted away: they would soon be earth and grass.

When the doctor departed for the city along with the visitors, we were again alone with Master Valdemar. He hadn't yet noticed the new girl. When he began again to fetch Hulda from the maid's room and the scraping under the rowan returned, I put on my wadmal trousers and lay on the nursery floor: if I whispered the words of Jesus, I could make all other sounds dissolve. I gripped the shovel's shaft, waiting for the night creature to visit me. When, finally, her furry face would come loose from the coal-dark corner, I almost stopped being afraid. Off and on, she'd sit in that corner, under the window or on top of the sideboard, her skinny girlish legs dangling like two pale, misshapen tallow candles in the darkness. She'd peer at me across the room with her glowing eyes, or sit and nod at me, friendly and encouraging, before flowing away again, quicksilver in the gloom.

And the slanting dawn light poured across the room, glinting off the discarded metal toys. Down in the kitchen, the sound of Fanny's morning movements at the stove would begin. Then I'd assemble the Scrawny One's instructions, those she issued from her coal-dark corner or from her place on top of the sideboard:

And the dragon made of fire came crashing down toward the woman, where she stood with the crown of stars around her head, crying out in childbirth. And the long tail of the beast swept the stars from the sky, down to the earth, as he waited by the woman to devour her child. But the woman fled into the desert, on eagle's wings. The dragon chased the woman and unleashed a flood from his mouth to wash her away. But the earth helped her, and a throne awaited the child in the city built of chalcedony and jasper, of emerald, beryl, and amethyst. And the desert became a plain of gold from which the woman would return to her child, who comes with her sceptre to cast the monster into the lake of fire. This is the second death.

FLOATING STREAKS OF WHITE in the blue sky.

I don't know exactly why I'd sit on the kitchen stairs, listening to little Beda as she muttered her made-up numbers over the pine cones. Why I insisted on going back to her when she never answered any of my questions and if, in any case, she was going to be taken away from me.

In a way, she did answer me: without looking at me, she would sometimes pause her counting for a moment if I happened to scratch my wooden clog on the floor while taking my seat, there on the top step. Her movements would slow. Or she would give me that glittering look across the kitchen table, a sign that she wasn't going to stop making a pig of herself just because Hulda and Gustava were grumbling.

So I sat down with her there at the back of the house, and her murmuring rose to the sky and formed an invisible dome, a shield of glass. I imagined that I could enter that dome, too, if only I kept her company for a while, and listened to her numbers, and let her mutter.

The early-morning light, mother of pearl. Dew on the summer grass, yet to be consumed by the heat of the day.

Doctor Eldh cut me out from the darkness, and he saved me from the gutter and he took me to Lilltuna, and he always brought new toys when he came: a small, turquoise-lacquered music box with a tulle-skirted ballerina; boxes of various sizes with marble lids; a green velvet notebook with its own padlock and key. I sat by the moss-covered vault in the garden, scratching my name on the stone with the chalk I'd been given for my slate; I lay on my back on the gazebo's verdigris roof. I let the evening sun play across my dress and my bare feet, soiled by the sodden earth. I still couldn't bear when the clouds left the sky and above me was vastness and emptiness: I'd put my bonnet over my face and clamp my eyes shut to keep out the unfathomable. My leash dangled from the knots I made Fanny tie around my waist, its end dragging in the grass below like a limp and feeble snake. In the garden I found stones and old shards of porcelain that I placed in the marble boxes; I searched the ground for traces of those who had come before; I dug up the small broken coffee cup handles from bygone picnics and gatherings in the bowers, turning them into treasures and ephemera that I placed in my dollhouse, among the tables and chairs and sconces in the snug, wallpapered rooms. I sat at the walnut table, opposite Doctor Eldh, and the smiles of his daughters from behind the glass in the oval picture frames, always careful what questions I asked.

Perhaps he'd simply longed for an outpost, for a girl to confide in. I came to know the nooks and crannies in the garden; I came to know the spellings for things, and to curtsy when I received my pat on the head from him on the front steps when he came back. And the doctor always did come back, until he didn't anymore.

After I took to the forest with Beda, the doctor waited a long time before returning to Lilltuna; more than two weeks went by. A punishment, I assumed, or perhaps it was because of that other, more intangible thing: a loss of interest, a boredom with it all. It had been a long time since the doctor had come with the dresses made of raw silk and velvet for my piano recitals. Perhaps he no longer knew what to make of me.

In the summer just gone, when he was last at Lilltuna, he

had often fallen asleep early. He'd collapse on the drawing-room sofa and fall into the heavy slumber that came with the punch or the sloeberry wine. Or he'd stagger into his chamber and close the door and not come out before the morning meal.

It could have been that the doctor did not in fact hear the badger that made its noises throughout those August nights, screaming as if it had been wounded by a shot or inexplicably gone mad. A tormented animal that Krantz would otherwise have silenced with his hunting rifle but that now, for some reason, he left alone, avoided, staying in the farmhand's cottage. The doctor slept; he closed the door to his chamber or sat nodding on the sofa when the scraping and thudding under the rowan began in the night. Now it was July. And the doctor was not awake on the evening when Master Valdemar went to find Beda for the first time. That night, he was not on the sofa but in his own bed, and he did not wake up, though the plodding of the master's untied boots echoed through the house, and the badger's cry unfurled between the trees.

Earlier that day the doctor had sat under the parasol out on the hill with the master, drinking afternoon tea. And the shadow had crossed the master's face: he had a slight tremble from a hangover as he raised his steaming cup to his lips with his slender fingers. Suddenly, little Beda came walking, down by the pasture, with water buckets for the animals yoked across her shoulders: and so at last the master noticed her. I was sitting with the *Flora* in the grass: out of the corner of my eye I saw how the master arrested the motion of his cup when he laid his eyes on her.

Perhaps he had simply tired of his nighttime diversions under the rowan tree, of Hulda's silenced warble, of the greyness that had inexorably settled over her face. Perhaps he preferred how it had been at the start, when she'd darted into the night's light in her woollen dress and he'd had to give chase for a while before catching her. It was hard to know what the master desired when the shadow took him. What he wanted and what he did not want, those evenings when he sat cackling and whining and sobbing to himself out in the garden chair, and then raging around at night in the library, crashing into the furniture. And when he went for Hulda, and pulled her off the maid's sofa, and pushed her through the house, out to the rowan tree, when the pressure became too strong. And when he suddenly lost interest. And wearied of it. Was it because it had become routine or was it the greyness, the docility in Hulda, that had replaced that first gloss of fear, the fear that had made her resist, but then made her fall silent and become peculiar, a grey hole of nothing, hanging there over the gruel? Maybe he simply tired of it or had changed his mind for no reason. And the sun was glinting so nicely on the hill when Beda appeared with the yoke. And the master arrested the motion of his cup, and he looked at her with those shimmering green eyes as she went to fetch the water. And then he raised the cup to his lips and took a sip of tea.

That evening, he fetched Beda. And the next morning Hulda sat eating the gruel in the kitchen with a fresh hunger. Just once, with a mixture of wonder and relief, she glanced up at little Beda, who was sitting opposite her on the bench, slurping with that mouth of hers as if nothing had happened.

And during the midday rest, Beda was back on the hill with the cones, as usual. The doctor left Lilltuna and came back; July passed. Whenever the shadows crowded the master's face, turning him tedious and incomprehensible, the doctor kept away for a few days, there in the city with his daughters and patients, so the master could be left alone to recover. I used to think that what the master was doing for the doctor was a form of work, like any other work that had to be done out at Lilltuna: the dawn milking and the chopping of the wood, the chicken plucking and the jam boiling, the fetching of the water from the well. And perhaps the master really was a tomcat who basked in the sunlight, an enviable creature who moved with ease among the night-eyed. The doctor continued to lean back on the drawing-room sofa; he watched the master with that delighted, submissive, sparkling gaze. And the brilliance of that gaze spun a thread in the air between them, a bond invisibly drawn between their bodies. The doctor came and left, and at her morning gruel Hulda now sat in relief, the greyness gone from her face. And at night it was Beda who was fetched from the maid's room and driven to the edge of the garden; I would hear her clap her hands together on her way down, and a muttering that rose between the claps. It only took the master a few smacks to silence her, and, in a deeper recess of the darkness, the badger's howl arose instead.

And this was just as well, and what harm did it do to someone like Beda; after all, in the daytime she'd still be sat out on the hill with the cones, undisturbed. And she continued to work, though the bruises spread up her neck and one eye became swollen. August came. In the thickets out in the garden, the lingonberries gleamed in the sun like drops of blood floating in the green. At night I recited Jesus's words, but still I heard Beda being dragged around, and the sliding down in the corridor as she was fetched and taken to the garden or pummelled into the field. And each time she'd clap in her peculiar way, and start up her muttering, and was silenced only after being given a smack. From the window I would see the two of them take shape, down there in the grey haze, while the master walked out of earshot with Beda, and then they'd be swallowed again by the garden's black leaves, or they'd melt away in the expanse of acres beyond: if I sharpened my gaze, I could discern the master's shirt down there in the pasture, a faint field of light hovering just above the ground before it, too, smeared into the night. The cows moved across the dead summer grass. Heavy bodies, shimmering and buoyant in the darkness. No wind. And the night became that furry body, rising from the shadows on a scrawny girl's legs with an unborn, animal face. Downstairs, Fanny shut her door, and Krantz kept to the farmhand's cottage. Except when, on the last evening, the dragging and crashing was louder.

That evening, I sat in the dark in the nursery with my broken shovel and the wadmal trousers on. When dawn came, I took them off and pushed the shovel under the bed. Then I went down to sit on the kitchen stairs as usual and waited for little Beda.

ON MY SEVENTH BIRTHDAY, Doctor Eldh gifted me a kite. It was red and made of a thin, silky, almost transparent paper pulled taut on a cross made of sticks. At one end of the cross hung a finely twisted kite string, which I gripped in one hand as I sat by the doctor in the carriage on the way to the crest of the hill, to let the kite loose in the wind. The doctor was happy and excited; he held the kite carefully between the fingers of both hands, and each time the carriage lurched, he raised it slightly above his knees to protect the delicate paper. The sky was clear blue, it was a hot August, the air over the field did not move.

All day long I ran beside the doctor with the kite, but no wind came. Out by the road, the hired coachman sat in the carriage he'd parked in the shade of a tree and watched us as we bounded and dashed around in an attempt to catch a bit of wind, me with the string in my hand and the doctor with the kite behind. Every time there was a slight breeze, the doctor released the kite, which lifted only briefly off the ground, then fell. The field tore the red paper and the doctor cursed. Endless blue above. Then, finally, the doctor broke the kite's wooden cross and he turned on his heel and walked himself back to the house, down through the field, paying no mind to the parked carriage. I stood on the crest, with summer's outstretched hills at my back, and the farms below stuck out like rust-red squares, their woodwork trims painted white and their chimneys smoking: the animals moving in the pasture were vanishing small dots on a mottled yellow bed. After a while, the coachman slapped his horse and came to fetch me. He put the kite on the seat beside me, along with a strip of the fragile paper that had been torn off during the last attempt at flight. He looked at me, curiously or with pity, before closing the door. When the carriage started moving, I grabbed the strip and held it out of the window. And suddenly the wind did blow: it snatched the strip from my hand, and the red wing flew.

It was night when I took Beda away with me: she was still in pain, and I had to force her through the forest down to the pond. This was after the evening when he who called himself Master Valdemar had suddenly risen from his garden chair, stumbled out into the pasture, and disappeared for hours. That evening, he did not come back until the thick, grainy summer night closed in around Lilltuna: he came back for Beda, or for something else that wasn't entirely clear. Before this, he'd been more unhinged than usual down in the library, twaddling nonsense for a long time in the armchair with his bottle before flying up and charging right out into the twilight. The evening he disappeared, his curls glistened in the last of the sun as he waded through the tall meadow grass toward the forest. I sat up in the window and watched him; I had put on my wadmal trousers, and when he was slow to return, I believed for a moment that it was over. That he'd sunk into some swamp or fallen into the pond or had left Lilltuna once and for all. But then I heard him downstairs, crunching across the gravel in the courtyard. How he thundered against the corridor walls on his way to the maid's room. There, he flung open the door and walked in, but he did not come back out with Beda as usual.

And perhaps it really was because of the badger's unexpected silence that I decided to go down and sit in the kitchen to wait for him. I was the Bandaged One: I had the lantern lit on the table and the shovel shaft ready in one hand, and I had to sit there in the kitchen for a long time and wait while the master carried on with Beda, inside the room where Hulda and Gustava were still there on the maid's sofa, as if he no longer cared who heard or saw. Through the wall, the thuds of Beda's body reached me as it hit the panels and slipped, as he worked his way through her. The shadows of the summer night on the trees in the garden. The magpies' rattling laughter.

Then I saw Krantz. His sudden appearance in the square of light on the stoop leading into the kitchen. He stood there on the bottom step, gripping the railing as if about to make a leap: as if he had suddenly woken up out there in the farmhand's cottage, or had been lying in the straw bed gathering his courage, and was finally here at the house to put a stop to it. He walked partly up the stoop, and then he halted and started to tread on the spot: he didn't go in. Krantz stood there, wavering and hesitating until he wasn't. Instead, he looked straight at me through the window glass, with something razor-sharp and naked and apologetic in his eyes. He stood for a while in the rippling lantern light, and then he lowered his gaze and let his shoulders drop. He turned on the steps, took himself out of the light, and returned to the farmhand's cottage, his back disappearing under the trees.

The lantern flickered, and the flame died.

When the door to the maid's room finally opened and I heard the master walk back through the house to the library, the trees outside were already as dark as pitch. It sounded as if he were barefoot: no plodding boots, and no Beda. I sat for a while in the kitchen with the shovel in my hand, the extinguished lantern on the table before me. Then I went up to the maid's room. Hulda and Gustava were lying on the sofa, silent, eyes wide open: the whites were shining and moving around in the dark. The air was thick and strange in there. Little Beda was sitting in the corner under the window, muttering; a strip of light from outside fell across her tousled hair and the dip of her temple, her lower body unclothed. I lifted her up and pulled on her skirt, saw in the darkness that she was bleeding from her buttocks as I led her out of the room's uneasy atmosphere of body and fear. In the kitchen entryway I held out Fanny's boots for her to step into.

By the time we reached the hill and began toward the water, Beda's muttering was unstoppable. The scent of autumn in the late summer night. Silver streaks between the spruces. The bogs open to the sky. She found it difficult to walk, slipping among the piles of rock and tumbling through the thickets; I flung out my shovel before me to clear a path, but the night made me lose my way, and at first I couldn't find the way to the pond. I tried to think of the black-haired sisters, of that summer when they'd walked, holding their picnic baskets, alongside the wheelbarrow in which I sat; I followed the curve of the earth and we wound down the densely overgrown forest slopes toward the water for what seemed like an eternity. Sometimes I thought I could see the girl creature in the distance ahead of us, with her skinny legs and encouraging face, its pallor among the bushes, showing us the way, urging us on: once I thought she held up her hand and waved to us. In the thickets below, the small night animals rustled, and further off between the trees moved flocks of deer; the pungent scent of the wild and of bird carrion settled in my nostrils.

In a patch of marsh, Beda fell down and lay there. I pulled her upright, but no more than that. She sat, her body heavy with reluctance, her muttering growing louder and more shrill. I began to pull at her arms and pressed myself with all my strength against her back to get her to move; I hissed her name and called her nasty things; I pulled her by the braids, which unravelled and were muddied by the earth. In the forest it was quiet now, no scrawny creature waving to show us the way, just the night's hollow bird cries and the endless slopes of trees, and when I reached for the shovel on the earth around me, it was nowhere to be found. With this I finally I sank down beside Beda and sat with her while the forest stayed silent and sealed. Beda continued to mutter, lost inside herself, and I thought that now the night would take us. But then I felt the shovel's hard shaft dig into my thigh, and I fumbled for a while along my trouser leg, soaked through from the marsh, until I got hold of it and could fish it out. Then I rose, and with the shovel I struck Beda's shoulder, once and with all my might. And she went quiet again, as she always did. When I took her by the elbows and pulled her up, she was obliging. The dawn mist between the trees, thinning to finally expose the water. White veils across its surface. The fox there on the other side before it slunk through the pines and disappeared. Below, the pond's unmoving eye was embedded in the bulrush and reeds and seemed to be looking at us. It was like in my dream, but without the fire.

The borrowed boots I'd laced Beda into in the dark entryway had sunk a bit into the moss on the rock where we stood. Now suddenly silent, she was clutching a young birch tree in the dawn light, as if to brace herself against the pain. *Just a little further,* I coaxed, offering her my hand. Her skirt was stained and rust-coloured at the buttocks. The sky strained above the water. There was the fleeting cry of waterfowl. Then the solar flame as it emerged from behind the treetops and the water's edge opposite, where a dense forest rose like a border. I pictured the landscape opening up behind it, becoming valleys and hills with moss-covered piles of rock and cottages and farms and tracks and railways and more forest and rivers and churches, and the networks of streets inside the cities with their harbours open onto the sea. We sat for a while on the rock there, at the edge of everything, while the sun rose in the sky and the bright light flashed around us, catching in the dew on the moss. Beda crumpled and was leaning against the birch now, her eyes shut, perhaps she was asleep. I pulled off her mud-caked boots, her skirt now soaking wet. No birds above the water. We had arrived. And yet we hadn't got anywhere.

Then we heard Krantz with the wheelbarrow on the hill. He had to work hard for a long time to pry my fingers from Beda, slapping the backs of my hands until I let her out of my arms. Deep blue sky above the trees. The smell of brown sludge rising from the stagnant water. Krantz took Beda by the waist and hoisted her onto the cart, his shirt dark with sweat as he transported her all the way back through the forest. The moisture dripped from her clothing where she hung over the edge of the barrow, and the muddy path squelched as I trudged behind Krantz. When we came to Lilltuna, Hulda and Gustava were processing the potatoes on the bench below the veranda. Looking at us.

Then I became the one Krantz transported; he carried me up the stairs to my nursery, Fanny behind us with the bedclothes pressed to her chest, her gaze elusive, and I stared at her over Krantz's shoulder, trying to understand.

The bandage was peeled off me, and I let go of the shovel as soon as they tried to take it from me, and Fanny and Hulda washed my body with wet rags. They dressed me in my sleeping gown and pantalettes and fed me oat soup. It was my twelfth birthday.

The thrushes in the rowan tree outside, daylight sweeping over the tiles. Gustava behind me, by the commode, saying my name. *Caesaria,* she said in that pleading tone, as if she wanted to comfort me or explain the unexplainable. But I didn't respond: I waited for the Scrawny One, for her to come back, I didn't turn around.

Snow now.

I've nailed the windows shut against the cold; I'm burning the last of the wood; I no longer go out. Through the velvet dark I hear animals prowling around the house, a lynx or a fox or runaway mongrels from the farms beyond the hill. Fierce fights flare up and then settle: sharp cries and bodies crashing into each other, then only the wind against the walls. I sleep briefly between waking, slowly eating dried meat, only small shreds: I wait.

Moonbeam.

When we were brought back from the pond, I lay under the horse blanket in my nursery for sixteen days while the doctor didn't come. When I heard the first carriage rattle into the courtyard, I heaved myself up in bed; I could see at once that the doctor wasn't there, only a coachman and a farmhand he must have sent from the city. Then I watched Krantz, who stood down on the hill, his hands driven into his pockets as, behind the coach box, the coachman and the farmhand packed Beda's belongings. She looked the same as when she'd arrived, though now with a laundered skirt and a clean face. I saw her braids fly across her back as the wagon lurched the corner, the cleft lip in her slightly crooked face. I saw her mouth move as if she were counting. All the way along the boundary of the garden and up the slope of the hill, I followed the carriage with my eyes. When it reached the crest, Beda suddenly turned back from the box next to the coachman and gave me and Lilltuna one last look. I thought about how she would fall silent for a moment when

I scraped my foot against the kitchen stairs, there with her pine cones around the back; I thought about her brown gaze as she slurped her gruel. Her face: now a white oval inside a dirt-brown shawl, far away in the field, indistinct and distant, as if she were standing on the far side of a lake. Then the carriage rounded the crest and was gone.

The second cab came a few days later, at dawn, again without the doctor. This time I stayed in bed in the nursery's gritty light. I heard the hired coachman lugging Master Valdemar's things downstairs. The master departed as quickly as he'd arrived, like a dream you blink away. Perhaps at last he'd recovered and so was leaving. Perhaps he was to resume his place by the fire in the Eldh city residence, to continue to converse and recount, and sip the hot punch, and, in the fire's heat, expound in great detail the beautiful and bewildering things of the continent for the daughters. Those long fingers would hold his cup in that feather-light way, and he wouldn't scald himself with the hot liquid; his countenance would be smooth and free from shadows after his long reinvigo-ration at the doctor's summer residence. Yes, perhaps there was no more to it. Like two clouds that flash in the bright sky, then slide together before disappearing, with the same inevitability and ancient ease with which seeds grow in the soil and become trees.

I listened to the coach door slam shut behind him, to the rattle of wheels and the clatter of hooves fading away. It was still dawn. Out in the pasture the cows were lowing; I imagined them rising from the grass out of the night.

Snow.

When the doctor at last came out to Lilltuna, after the sixteen days he'd let pass, he walked up the stairs to my nurs-ery with dragging steps. He entered and sat in the armchair by the foot of the bed. He had with him a belated birthday gift in a little box with gold ribbons, which he set at my feet on top of the horse blanket. Silence at first. The lingering scent of pond in my nostrils. The cane creaking under the doctor's great elbows. He cleared his throat, savouring his words, turning them over in his mouth as if they were made of sugar, before once again recounting the story of my Creation. He told me about his scrawny one, how she stood in the rain outside the lying-in hospital, and about the unprecedented operation: *One of the first of its kind,* as he used to say. The opening of the abdomen, the spurt of blood, the girl's indifferent yellow eyes skidding over the walls: how he then brought me into the world. I still imagine how his face would have looked in the mirror, there in the city on that day long ago, when I was plucked from the darkness. Blue eyes below thick eyebrows, mutton chops in tufts along the jawline. The September sky on its way to October.

The doctor did as he always had when he told the story: he made the words sound unused, as new as baby birds, but I could hear a hollow clang behind them now: a different tone of voice, a hint of boredom or untruth, a weariness with what he was saying. His big face glistened a little in the light from where I could see it, rising above my feet and the little gold-ribboned birthday present, as he thoughtfully tapped his steepled fingers. I tried to determine the moment when he must have tired of Lilltuna: whether it was before his long tour, when he stopped bringing the toys I'd put on the wish list and forgot about the new skates for the winter, or whether it was because of my morbid disposition. Or had it in fact occurred much earlier, when I was still a small child in a smock: when I still sat in the library under the East Indian wall clock, awaiting my lessons, or ran out to him on the front steps in my summer shoes; when he'd lift me high above his head and spin me round and round in the air.

The grey light fell across the toys and the abandoned desk. The doctor got up from his chair. He didn't look me in the eye when he grabbed my toes through the horse blanket to give them an encouraging shake, then he went down to the coach again and departed. That was the last time he came out to Lilltuna.

A short while into November, I watched Hulda and Gustava from the nursery window, heading straight across the field into the raw cold of dawn. They'd packed the bundles they'd arrived with and hung them on their backs; they darted through the furrowed field; they didn't turn around. There was a narrow strip of light over the spruce tops as they rounded the crest and were gone. Stars at the edge of the sky.

After Hulda and Gustava stole away, no new girls were brought to Lilltuna: only Krantz and Fanny and I were left in those final few years. The cows were sold off, just two of the red ones kept for milk, along with some sheep and the chickens. I grew large and hairy; I wore Fanny's cast-off dresses; the boils grew heavy under my blouse and I let them hang; when Fanny became too tired for her chores, I began to fetch wood from the shed and tend the chickens. The chucks would bluster in their cages when I entered the henhouse; if one of them slipped away on the hill where I took them for the chop, I let her run. Grimy yellow wings flapping far off in the field. I never asked Fanny if a message had come from the city and Doctor Eldh, I never asked any questions that might burden her; I let her take care of me without any fuss for as long as she could, and after that I took care of myself. She'd sit huddled on the bench on the veranda with her cardigan around her shoulders, looking like a skinny crow as she chewed her tobacco and watched the dusk clouds sail by. Krantz still drove into town and bought her the pungent-smelling black pulp with the money she'd saved in the box on the mantelpiece. Was that money the old maintenance Krantz would pick up from the Eldh residence in the city? I don't know, but Krantz's purchases became ever more frugal, and when he returned in the carriage, the sacks would be only half-full. The piebald died, the dapple grey remained. I can picture Krantz standing in the barn, brushing her with long sweeping strokes in the light from outside.

I walked in the garden and picked the fruit from the trees and put it in the birchbark basket I'd strapped to my back; I pickled the pears for Fanny and let her sit in the drawing-room and eat preserves by the fireplace. When the monthly blood arrived, I simply let it run down my thighs and into my clogs. I still made loop braids, then I started not to. I took the hunting rifle into the forest with Krantz and learned to shoot small birds; we never went as far as the pond. I became a good shot, going to the forest alone, and when I would return with a clutch of pigeons hanging from my belt, Krantz would watch me from the edge of the pasture, Doctor Eldh's old casquette on his head to shield him from the rain. He'd raise his hand and wave. A mother-of-pearl arc twinkled in the sky above the roof of the house as the grey clouds dispersed.

The image of Lilltuna as a forgotten nursery would come to me sometimes; on my way back from hunting, the gazebo would remind me of a dollhouse that someone had tired of, outgrown and left behind, with its white-lacquered pillars and verdigris roof peeking out from the vegetation. It was only up close that you could you see that the wood was cracked and flaking and consumed by rot. At last, one side of the gazebo collapsed, and shortly afterwards the roof of my nursery began to leak and I moved in with Fanny in the kitchen for good. She'd sit in the rattan armchair I'd dragged down the stairs from the nursery and placed by the wood-burning stove, stirring the embers with her rake; her hands were dry and thin, the tobacco in her cheek a lump in an otherwise hollowed, aged face.

The thunder passing over the spring slopes.

The yellow light between the poplars when the rain eased.

In the kitchen that final winter, Fanny lay in bed, wheezing grimly into the small hours, her back bony through the nightgown, and when I clasped her hand it was ice-cold and unresponsive. It was January when Krantz finally packed her into the sleigh under several layers of blankets and furs to seek help in the city for her cough. Her face was as small as a child's, peeking out from the fur, and it looked at me questioningly, or was it sadly, with its feverish eyes. Wearing her old winter coat, I stood on the kitchen steps and held the lantern for Krantz in the morning darkness; the snow was deep around the house, except where I'd helped to shovel it away so he could take out the sleigh. The landscape radiated strangely once he was sat on the box, and he smacked the dapple grey, and the sleigh dashed up the hill. No snowfall. Stinging cold.

I waited three weeks for Krantz and Fanny, then I waited no more.

I shovelled the snow from the path to the barn so I could milk the two remaining cows, my hands so chapped by the cold that the first one shied away when I grabbed her teats. I let the warm milk run down the beet-red fingers of one hand before switching to the other. I heard the lynx out on the hill, slinking between the outbuildings.

I started sleeping in the library by the fireplace; I let the cats into the house; I chopped the head off one of the last chickens and slowly ate the roasted meat under the wall clock in my winter coat; I waited for the Scrawny One, for the Night from which she would return. I still kept the rope tied around my belly, just below the hanging boils; I let it drag behind me as I walked the grounds, like an animal tail or a poisonous snake, and it became caked in mud and then sandy grey and stiff.

Toward March the winterfeed ran out.

The cows called out to me at night from the barn, and the last sheep bleated shrilly from inside their pen. At last, I went out and released them, let them trot out across the frosty field and onto the main road.

After that, it took a couple of hours before people came; through the window I immediately recognized the farmer who had come to the mating with one of the yearlings long ago. I'd extinguished the fire behind me so there'd be no chimney smoke. The farmer and the farmer's men walked carefully and hesitantly into the courtyard; they knocked on the door at the front and the one at the kitchen entrance. They stamped the snow off their boots before entering the farmhand's cottage, the shed with the mangle, the hen-house, and then the barn, where they took two sheep that had returned to the pen from the field although I'd released them. The men tied the sheep with the ropes they'd brought with them, wrapped around their waists. Then they went after the last hens, still caged in the henhouse, putting them in grain sacks they'd brought along and tying them up. The hens screamed and flapped inside the sackcloth. The farmer's eyes searched the house's windows before he left with the sheep and the sacks of hens and the men. Their thick brown coats got smaller and smaller the further along the crest they went, and I could see their little cold-red faces shining under their caps as they turned around one last time before going over.

Black lashes of forest tore into the sky as the afternoon darkness drew in.

I slept with the hunting rifle beside me and the rope tied around my waist; I dropped rocks into the well to break the ice; I lit the stove with what was left of the wood, not caring about the smoke that billowed against the creamy sky above the house. No one came to Lilltuna until late spring.

I spent my time sat in the library on the ottoman, wrapped in the horse blanket I'd dragged down from the nursery, which was otherwise untouched, the toys in their boxes and the commode shut, and of course I had the rattan armchair down here, which I'd carried down for Fanny in her last days at Lilltuna. I never went back up there, though sometimes I heard dripping from the roof and imagined the rot in the tiles that would soon seep through the house.

I lined my clothes with straw from the barn, avoiding that now-unfamiliar face reflected in Krantz's mirror shard, which still hung there on the nail as I passed by. I chopped up the rattan chair and used it for fuel, I threw the doctor's manuscripts into the fireplace one by one; the papers curled in the embers, and I could no longer tell whether it was the doctor's handwriting or my own that covered those old worn pages. The smell of burning ink mingled with the pungent smell of piss from the bucket I'd placed in the corner and the stench of feces and cat that had begun to settle in the walls. The cats had taken up residence upstairs, and I would hear them bounding across the floor at night; maybe they were avoiding me or had realized I had no food to offer them. One morning I heard a cat giving birth right above my head, but when I got up a few hours later, one of the others had already gnawed the kittens to death: they lay curled up and motionless at the top of the stairs, next to the door.

I no longer touched the square piano; I twisted my hair into a whip and tucked it under the doctor's casquette that Krantz had left behind, long now and smelling of tallow and dirt and premature old age. Golden dusk. The heat rising slowly from the earth made the entire estate smell of decay and the smell that accompanies a birth. I ate from the bottom of the bag of oats; I cupped my hands and submerged them

178

in the enamel bucket I'd drawn from the well, and the ice-cold water made my eyes tear up as I drank. It was May by the time the cab from the city arrived.

I was sitting in the library when I heard the carriage rattling on the driveway, and had stopped lighting the stove because the wood in the shed had run out and summer was on its way. I placed myself behind the velvet curtains at the window. The coachman wore a tall hat and was dressed grandly, sat on the box and holding the reins of two silver-grey horses; he wore gloves and a cravat and his shoes hardly had any dust on them when he climbed down to open the coach door for the two ladies who stepped into the midday sun. They let down their summer-coloured dresses and opened their parasols and adjusted the curls at the edges of their bonnets, blinking a little at the sun with their round, porcelain-white faces before letting their light-blue eyes glide curiously over the house. I recognized them at once from behind the glass ovals on the doctor's desk, though they were no longer children in summer hats but grown women. They walked into the garden, not entering the house, and their voices were chattering and noisy; I noticed that one of the doctor's daughters was slightly larger than the other as they walked around looking at the collapsed gazebo and the splintering pasture fence and the English garden that had gone to seed. They pointed with delight as a fawn ran after its mother across the field's overgrown furrows, startled by the ruckus when the coachman's foot went right through one of the veranda steps. The wood was rotten through and through, and the coachman had to sit on the hillside for a long time rubbing his injured foot.

All day long the daughters walked round and assessed Lilltuna; they'd brought food and refreshments with them and they sat down for lunch in the old garden furniture, taking out paper and writing instruments and seeming to be calculating something. I could feel my mouth water and hunger tug at my belly, and at last they entered the house through the veranda, though the coachman repeatedly advised them not to. Through the library window I saw them grasp the hems of their dresses and remove their bonnets. I heard how gingerly they stepped across the bowed drawing-room floor, their prim feet laced into spring boots. The light was waning, I was standing in the darkness of the library, and now the hour had come: one of the daughters let out a screech, and I understood that it was the stench and the cats, and they both hurried out to the veranda again, their handkerchiefs pressed to their faces. With their gloved fingers they grasped the coachman's supportive hands, one by one, as they stepped over the hole left in the stairs by his foot.

I stood at the window as they got into the carriage, and the driver slammed the door and clacked at the horses before driving along the edge of the garden up the hill. The daughters never returned to Lilltuna.

Bright red evening sky, no clouds.

I devoured the leftovers in the forgotten basket on the garden table; I slept next to the rifle while the cats pounced and chased each other upstairs. Hot, stagnant summer days. With my back to the glimmering sunshine outside the library windows, I moved the hands in the right direction around the dial inside the wall clock: the machinery sprung and clicked, and small flakes of gold from the case rained down on my hands.

Every now and then some children from the farms would sneak into the courtyard; I'd stand behind the curtain in the library window, watching them play and hide in the barns and climb and hang in the fruit trees in the garden under the blue July and August skies. Sometimes they made away with Krantz's old straw bales in the barn, loading them onto the rusty old wheelbarrow and driving it across the field while howling in triumph. Watery eyes, mousy hair under summer caps.

When the gunpowder ran out, I fashioned a bow. I plucked a string from the square piano and fixed it to a frame, practising archery with one of my slates nailed to a linden as a target board. I became quick with the bow. I shot sparrow and mouse and rabbit; I skinned and plucked my prey and roasted it in the wood stove that I lit with Fanny's matchsticks. Eggshell sky. Swarms of gnats. As the evenings grew cooler, I tore down the velvet from one of the windows and wrapped myself in it. In August the matches ran out: I made a fire with the doctor's magnifying glass, which I held under the sun until the wood began to burn, and when the autumn rains came I went without food for days.

In September I once again heard the rattle of a cab on the road and I barricaded myself in the woodshed, behind the peephole that the children from the farms would poke their fingers and straw through when they came to visit. Waiting. I saw Krantz walk into the courtyard, no sign of the cab. He wore a dark blue jacket that was new to me, the elbows patched. He went into the house and up the stairs, and I watched him looking out the nursery window for a while. Heard him shooing the cats. Then he came back out and zigzagged his way around the property. Calling my name. I was pressed against the peephole, my breath burning around my face. Finally he went into the barn, and the barnyard with the abandoned box stalls and the open pen. Then he came out and stood on the hillside by the woodshed, a few metres from me. His back was turned, he spat some tobacco on the ground, his body looked tense under his new clothes: he was listening for something. He repeated my name but more softly. I put my palm to the closed door, the wood cold and damp; I could have simply pushed it open and made myself known. Then someone shouted from the other side of the house, a comrade or a coachman he'd brought with him. I stood there with my hand on the wooden door; I didn't push it open. Krantz lingered in the silence for a few moments, then walked slowly through the wild grass in the direction of his comrade's shouts. An evening cuckoo. I waited in the woodshed until I could no longer hear the carriage on the road; I went inside and to sleep in the nest I'd made in the library; at dawn I watched through the window as the sun's glowing orb rose, until the room was bathed in red. When the mornings were cold, I'd run my hand under my skirts and put my finger on the burning lump above the slit and close my eyes, rubbing gently.

I picked the locks on the drawers in the walnut table and took out the things that Doctor Eldh had left behind: small pipes and tobacco so dry it crumbled to black dust between my fingers; a cracked pince-nez; the writing instruments and the dried-up ink and a pair of old summer gloves. In the last drawer was the cardboard box containing the pelvic bone, still labelled *No. 38*. I laid out the objects so I could see them; I fastened the small bone around my neck with yarn I had unravelled from Fanny's winter cardigan; I let the mosquitoes bite me until they bit me no more. I went hunting with the bow in the forest behind the field, at the outer limits of Lilltuna. I never went down to the pond to fish. I ate lean rabbit meat that I roasted on an open fire behind the house under the linden. The skins would turn sooty, and when I wiped my face with the back of my hand after my meal, it turned a greasy black.

Autumn ended, a winter came, several springs.

In the summers I sometimes rose in the muggy night air and walked barefoot under the trees in the garden, the rope wrapped tightly around me under my clothes; I'd cut across the field and I'd round the crest of the hill and approach the farms where occasionally candles burned in the windows, even into the small hours, the night birds circling overhead. I thought about the children inside the cottages, drinking warm milk or squabbling with their siblings and getting combed for lice and braiding their hair by the hearths and stoves and fireplaces while the dogs lay on their porches and stared into the darkness, their heads resting on their paws. I wove between the barns and slunk along their walls to see if I could snatch something edible or of value; I kept away from the animals that stood guard and got better at moving with silent steps: I always returned to Lilltuna by dawn.

ABOUT THE AUTHOR

HANNA NORDENHÖK has been awarded several major literary honours for her work. Her novel *Caesaria* (2020) won Swedish Radio's Literary Prize and was shortlisted for Tidningen Vi's Literature Prize. Nordenhök also works as a translator from Spanish and has been praised for her translations of Fernanda Melchor, Andrea Abreu, and Gloria Gervitz. She lives in Stockholm.

PHOTO: ELVIRA GLÄNTE

ABOUT THE TRANSLATOR

SASKIA VOGEL is the author of the novel *Permission* and a translator of more than twenty Swedish-language books. Her writing has been awarded the Berlin Senate Endowment for Non-German Literature. Her translations have won the Bernard Shaw Prize (Johanne Lykke Holm's *Strega*), been shortlisted for the PEN Translation Prize (Jessica Schiefauer's *Girls Lost*), and been supported by grants from the Swedish Arts Council, the Swedish Authors' Fund, and English PEN. She was Princeton's Translator in Residence in fall 2022 and lives in Berlin.

PHOTO: FETTE SANS

COLOPHON

Manufactured as the first North American edition of *Caesaria*
In the fall of 2024 by Book*hug Press

Copy-edited by Stuart Ross
Proofread by Laurie Siblock
Type + design by Malcolm Sutton

Cover photos: Augusta Modén by A.W. Eurenius & P.L. Quist / public
domain; cloudy sky by Free Nature Stock / public domain

Printed in Canada

bookhugpress.ca